CC

THE
THUNDERING
TRAIL

THE THUNDERING TRAIL

Norman A. Fox

Thorndike Press • Chivers Press
Thorndike, Maine USA   Bath, Avon, England

This Large Print edition is published by Thorndike Press, USA and by Chivers Press, England.

Published in 1996 in the U.S. by arrangement with Richard C. Fox.

Published in 1996 in the U.K. by arrangement with the author's estate.

U.S. Hardcover   0-7862-0584-9   (Western Series Edition)
U.K. Hardcover   0-7451-3917-5   (Chivers Large Print)

Thorndike Large Print ® Western Series.

The text of this Large Print edition is unabridged.
Other aspects of the book may vary from the original edition.

Set in 16 pt. News Plantin by Rick Gundberg.

Printed in Great Britain on permanent paper.

British Library Cataloguing in Publication Data available

Library of Congress Cataloging in Publication Data

Fox, Norman A., 1911–1960.
    The thundering trail / Norman A. Fox.
    p.   cm.
    ISBN 0-7862-0584-9 (lg. print : hc)
    1. Large type books.   I. Title.
[PS3511.O968T48   1996]
813'.54—dc20   95-42202

THE
THUNDERING
TRAIL

Chapter One

When he loped into the ranch yard, he halted his horse beneath the tall locust tree, sitting his saddle for a full minute and letting his eyes dwell upon the familiar things, just as a hungry man might tantalize himself with the sight of food long delayed, before falling to the feast. The breeze tonight was like a woman's hand, soft and gentle, and a West Texas moon hung aloft, brushing magic upon the corrals and sheds, making the sprawling adobe ranch house glimmer ghostly and shapeless in the semi-gloom. All these things were as they'd been on a thousand nights like this one, yet tonight there was a difference, indefinable and somehow ominous.

Frowning, Chan Loring gazed toward the bunkhouse and found the cause of his concern, for the voices that came through the darkness were low and subdued where always they'd been loud and reckless, full of high spirits and carefree camaraderie. And by such a token he knew that something had come to the great Loring Lazy-L that had not been here before, and that its coming was a black swath of

7

shadow upon the place.

He stepped down from his saddle then, and the man who materialized to meet him, moving forward out of the gloom, peered long and intently, a gnarled little gnome with a lyre-shaped, tobacco-stained moustache and legs fashioned to fit a saddle.

"Chan," he cried, but his whoop of recognition was only an echo of what it might have been. "You've got back, boy. Thunder on the Pecos, but you're good for these eyes of mine."

"And it's grand to be home, you old hellion," Chan said, and gave his hand to Billy Wing, Lazy-L straw boss. "But has this outfit got religion while I've been up to Montana? It's quiet as a prayer-meeting hereabouts. How's the King?"

"King Loring's in the house," Billy Wing said. "I wish I knew an easier way of breakin' it to you, Chan. He come home tonight with a bullet in him. We did all we could for him, but he ordered us out of the house afterwards. Pete Still has rode into Rawson to fetch the sawbones."

"God!" Chan said, and put his shoulders against the saddle for support. "Who did it, Billy?" But Billy Wing could only shake his grizzled head.

"Is Mitch here?" Chan asked.

8

"Mitch ain't changed none since you left," Wing said bluntly. "He's probably in Caesar Rondeen's Spur Wheel Saloon swillin' rot-gut likker while his paw's maybe dying. I told Pete Still to tell him how things stood if he spotted Mitch, but not to waste no time lookin' for him."

Turning, Chan strode toward the ranch house, old Billy bowlegging along beside him as far as the front porch. Then Chan was in the big, lamp-lighted living room, where mesquite crackled in the fireplace and a scattering of straight-backed chairs made for hominess. But he stopped here only long enough to lay a consoling hand upon the shoulder of the fat, wailing squaw who'd been housekeeper as long as Chan could remember, then passed into the bedroom where King Loring lay, white as the pillow that bolstered him.

"King," Chan said. "King, old-timer —"

"Chan!" King Loring grinned, and extended his hand. "Weeks now we've watched the trail for sign of you, but that makes no never mind. You're here. Come closer, my boy, and let me look at you!"

They were a lot alike, these two, with their lean, highboned faces and their cobalt eyes — so much alike that those who didn't know that Chan had become a Loring by virtue of the King's generosity, always presumed they were blood kin. Yet some of their resemblance was because Texas had fashioned them, for men born to the saddle grow slab-muscled, and the Texas sun gives them a whang-leather hue.

But they were different, too, different as the buffalo and the longhorn — the one, Boone Loring, known to most as King Loring, stolid and shaggy, the other, Chan Loring, tough and rangy as the cattle that roamed the cedar brakes. Now King Loring was a stricken buffalo, yet the look of him was somehow reassuring, giving the lie to Billy Wing's fears, taking the edge from Chan's dread that all that must be said must be spoken at once.

"Who did this to you, King?" he asked. "I've got to know."

But the King waved a bloodless hand. "That can wait. Tell me first — did you find it?"

"I found it, King. I found your Whispering Basin up there beyond the Yellowstone, and it's like you remembered it — grass to brush a man's stirrups, and water a-plenty, and hills to shelter your herds when the blizzards blow. It's the kind of range West Texas used to have before every fool one of us overstocked so we could sell more cattle in the north. And it's yours, King, legally. I filed by proxy in your name and took up adjoining dummy claims in the names of the crew."

10

"Then we'll be moving to Montana pronto," King Loring decided. "The Lazy-L's got a new chance — north."

"I stopped off at Fort Faraday on the Yellowstone," Chan went on. "They gave me a beef contract for our older stuff — a contract that will give us money to establish ourselves in Whispering until we put tallow on the young beef. That soldier beef has got to be delivered by the middle of August, but we can make it easy."

" 'Easy?' " King Loring murmured. "You might as well have the straight of it, boy. Caesar Rondeen will see that nothing the Lazy-L does will be easy."

"Caesar Rondeen," Chan echoed, and suspicion built a flame in his cobalt eyes. "You mean that the old Loring-Rondeen feud has flared to life again? Then that's how you come to stop a bullet —"

"Wait," the King ordered. "Hear me out, Chan. There's so damn' much you've got to know, seein' as the big job will be your'n if this slug keeps me in bed for a long spell. You're twenty-two now, Chan, about the same age as Mitch, the way I've always figgered it. Twenty of those years you've packed my name, ever since the day I found you squawlin' in the ruins of a wagon train up in Comanche country."

11

"I know," Chan said humbly.

"I've always tried to give you the same end of the stick as Mitch," the King went on, "even if he is my flesh and blood and you're not. But maybe I ain't been fair some'eres along the line. You've never lied to me, Chan, which is more'n I can say for my other son. Don't lie to me now. How do I stand with you, boy?"

There was a deadly earnestness in the old man's tone. Something stuck in Chan's throat, and the words had to come around it. "Aces high, King," he managed. "I figgered you knew that."

The old cattleman relaxed against his pillow, his eyes half closed. "It was a long time ago," he said, a man seeing yesterday. "Four of us Texas cowpokes — me and Angus McQuade and the two Rondeen brothers, Slade and Caesar — took a *pasear* to Montana. It was snow-flyin' time when we looked on Whispering Basin, and I know that every man of us had the same thought — here was cow paradise. But folks in them days believed cattle couldn't winter in Montana."

"But they can," Chan protested.

The King nodded. "I know," he said. "And when the four of us turned south again, each of us was thinkin' that maybe someday we'd own that basin. Me, I married the gal that

12

was Mitch's mother — God rest her soul — and went to help Jeff Davis with his chores. Angus McQuade went into the army too, and afterwards drifted into Mexico, I heard tell. The Rondeens stayed in Texas . . ."

"— and Slade Rondeen became the dirtiest rustler in the brush country," Chan supplemented. "I've heard a heap of yarns about him, King. While most Texans was fighting for the Confederacy, skunks like him built up herds with a running iron, robbing their neighbors who were off doing the fighting. It was a purty, the way you trailed him down after the war and put a slug into him."

King Loring winced, and Chan strained his ears for the hoofbeats that would tell him Pete Still had arrived with the doctor.

"Most folks figgered Slade Rondeen had a killin' comin' to him," King Loring conceded. "But Caesar Rondeen showed up afterwards to even the score. When me'n Caesar matched smoke, I drove a bullet into the frame of the doorway where he was hunkerin', and a splinter of wood knocked out his left eye. He's hated my guts since, and when he started his Spur Wheel Saloon in Rawson, it didn't make us any friendlier. I ain't never set myself up as guardian of the morals of my crew, but I liked seeing them get a fair shake when they spent their pay. Rondeen's whiskey is poison, his decks are marked, and his wheels are fixed. And those gunnies of his'n, Doc Menafee and Jube Cazborg, see that nobody kicks too hard after they've been trimmed."

"Then it *was* Rondeen who put a slug into you tonight."

The King's fingers closed on Chan's wrist. "Hear the rest of it," he begged. "Yes, Caesar Rondeen and me matched smoke on the trail from Rawson to the Lazy-L a few hours ago. But don't go gunning for him, Chan. You see, there's two things that's got to be done, and I'm countin' on you to do them, and you'll be no good dead. Mitch ain't the son I've wanted him to be, Chan. He drinks too much, and he gambles, and he goes on too many trips to God knows where. He's young and wild and he'll outgrow all that. But it's you I'm depending on, Chan, to see that the spread gets a new start in Whispering. And I'm depending on you for something else —"

"All you've got to do is name it," Chan said softly.

"Caesar Rondeen owns a little black metal box, one of those things a gent uses to protect important papers from fire. He showed it to me tonight. Get it, Chan. And when you get it, destroy what's inside it without looking at them papers. It's a queer request to your way of thinkin', but that's the other thing I want

14

you to do. And promise me you won't match smoke with Rondeen."

"But you said he'd be buckin' the Lazy-L. If he tries to stop us from shovin' north — ?"

"He'll try." King Loring declared. "With half of Texas moving north, the game's played out here for all of us. The day has come when Rondeen's rememberin' Whispering. Besides, he hates the Lorings enough to want that grassland just to keep us from getting it. He'll try to stop you — shore. But you can't kill him, Chan. Do you savvy?"

"No, I don't," Chan countered. "But I'll run the show the way you want, King. And I'll get that black box."

"Good." The King sighed. "I'm puttin' things in your hands, boy. And I'll tell you anything I dare tell you."

Chan's brows came together, forming a puzzled V, and he sorted words, seeking the right ones.

"Once, when me and Mitch was kids, he taunted me about not really being a Loring. Up until then I'd sorta supposed we was some kind of cousins, but I asked you about it. You told me about finding that burned wagon train and bringing me home to be a brother to Mitch, seeing as we was about the same age. That's all I've ever needed to know, King. But now I'm wonderin' if there wasn't some

15

clue — something a man could get hold on to figure out my real name?"

King Loring smiled. "When a man starts worryin' about his family tree, he's either goin' into politics, or he's fallen for some filly. You meet a gal on the trail up to Montana, Chan? Is that it?"

"Yes," Chan nodded. "The girl I aim to marry. She's half-Spanish and half-Scotch, and the last time I saw her she was throwing bullets at me and daring me to come back. You've laid the cards out for me, King. I won't try to fool you. Angus McQuade's already in Whispering, backed by a bunch of small ranchers. He brought his daughter out of Mexico, and him and Consuelo are going to be hard to budge. But he made the mistake of squatting instead of filing, so he has no legal claim."

"McQuade," the King said, and took the news lightly enough. "Stubborn as Scotland himself, he is. Twenty-odd years him and me and Caesar Rondeen has dreamed the same dream, and now, with the big fight buildin' up, I — But you asked me a question, Chan. I can't help you none on that clue business, but it makes no never mind. A man is what he's shaped to be, and I'm thinkin' I did a good job on you — a better one than I did on Mitch. You're Chan Loring — old King

16

Loring's cub, and don't ever forget it. And that's name enough."

"Name enough," Chan agreed, and fell silent, thinking of many things, all of them tied to the Lazy-L and to this man who'd wrested a kingdom from the cactus, building an empire in the brush country, only to see his range turned dry and dusty, betraying him. And somewhere in Chan's reverie, he was jerked from it by the drumming of hoofs.

He glanced at King Loring then, seeing a change so slight as almost to defy the eye. And then Chan knew that only sheer will had sustained the man these past minutes, and that the King's every act and every word had been part of a play designed to hide the real extent of his hurt.

"King!" he cried, but there was no answer, and there'd never be an answer, so he slowly drew a blanket over the fixed features. Then he went to the porch to see lanky Pete Still helping Rawson's medico from a saddle.

"Tell the doc there's no work for him here," Chan said stonily to Billy Wing. "The King is dead. And me, I've got business in Rawson."

Billy Wing gave him a glance, and there must have been something in the stern set of Chan's jaw that told the oldster all he needed to know.

"Wait," Billy cried. "Sittin' here on the porch beneath the window, I couldn't help but hear all that you and King Loring palavered about. And yet you figger on facing Caesar Rondeen tonight. It's writ all over your face. Do you think Rondeen or Doc Menafee or Jube Cazborg made any promises not to smoke *you?*"

But Chan Loring was already heading for his horse, a grim determination manifesting itself in his lengthened stride. Muttering something that might have been a curse or a prayer, Billy Wing hurried after him.

Chapter Two

of easing down the gunsiter.

"Why did the King ride alone tonight?" he demanded, beery voice raised incredible way shuffling, heavy-voiced he had pushed it. Yet he cast that choice into hoodism hunting him.

The trail that led southward to Rawson was a twisted snake of silver beneath the moon, the shadows of scrub oak and tall mesquite like so many dark, wavering fingers seeking a hold upon it where the range was hilly. Across the miles Chan Loring and Billy Wing rode, each silent with his own thoughts, each wrapped in bitterness and grief, until a score of compelling questions came to Chan's tongue, refusing to be denied.

He was on his way to face Caesar Rondeen, just as Billy Wing had guessed, yet Chan had not so quickly forgotten his promise to the dying King. There could be no showdown for Chan, or at least not the sort he longed to have — gun against gun, with an old score wiped out to the resounding crash of them. ". . . you can't kill him, Chan," King Loring had decreed, and the promise Chan had made, tied his own gun hand. But there'd be war just the same, the old Loring-Rondeen feud flaring again, with another Loring carrying on where the King had left off. Chan Loring was at least going to have the scant satisfaction of tossing down the gauntlet.

"Why did the King ride alone tonight?" he demanded aloud. "He knew trouble was building. Every word he said proves it. Yet he took that chance with Rondeen hunting him."

"Me and the King loped into Rawson about sundown," Billy explained. "I was gonna hang around till he was ready to hit the home trail, but he just the same as ordered me to go on to the spread. Said he had a mite o' business to transact, and he headed for Whiskey Jenny's shack. The next time I saw King Loring, he come ridin' into the ranch yard, hours later, with blood on his saddle."

Chan twisted around abruptly. "Whiskey Jenny's," he said. "You trying to say that the King had gone in for having his fortune told? What in hell else would he be going to see that booze-swilling old woman for?"

Billy Wing shrugged. "The King did lots o' things that didn't make *sabe* to me," he admitted. "So long as I drawed ridin' pay from him, I never asked no questions. And what I've saw, I've kept to myself."

Chan turned these statements over in his mind, giving them the full weight of his consideration, and choosing his own words carefully.

"There's a moon tonight, but it don't light

the trail *I'm* trying to follow, Billy," he said. "You claim you heard the palaver between me and the King, so you know I've got two jobs to do. But the trail ahead is mighty tangled. If you can point any part of the way, I'm listenin'."

Silence . . . the clip-clop of hoofs . . . the music of spurs and bit chains . . . the uneasy creak of saddle leather — these things endured for an interminable length until Billy Wing spoke.

"I started riding for King Loring just about the time everybody was backslappin' him for burnin' down Slade Rondeen," Billy said. "Whiskey Jenny was hereabouts then. Something some folks don't know is that she was Slade Rondeen's wife. She'd been a dance hall gal down San Antone way, and she was mighty pretty afore she took to boozing. Ever since she was widdered, she's kept a-goin' straight down the greased skids to hell, drifting from town to town, and makin' a few dollars with her fortune telling. But she always comes back to Rawson — maybe because Slade's buried there."

"I remember seeing her around ever since I was a kid," Chan said. "But the King — ?"

"The King made it a habit to go see her ever so often, Chan. You didn't know that, eh? But you recollect that time seven-eight years back when he busted a laig out in the breakin' corral? The sawbones kept him outa the saddle for quite a spell, and durin' that spell he sent *me* in to see Whiskey Jenny — to take a package to her."

"A package?"

"Thunder on the Pecos, Chan, but I never meant to know what was in that package, believe me. But that boogery broomtail I was forkin' shied at his own shadow on the trail, and spilled me hard. I'd stuck the package in my chaps pocket, and since it was only wrapped in brown paper, one corner busted open when I lighted. There was greenbacks inside, Chan, a heap of them. Greenbacks which I delivered to Whiskey Jenny, and never got so much as a thank yuh."

"Money." Chan cried in surprise. "You mean the King's been paying Whiskey Jenny money all these years? That he went tonight to give her some? But maybe the King felt sorry for her, seein' as he'd made her a widow. That would have been like King Loring. He was soft as putty, in spite of all his bellowing. But if Whiskey Jenny was Slade Rondeen's wife, then she's Caesar's sister-in-law. He's fixed well enough to keep her from living on charity."

Billy Wing shrugged. "I've told yuh this for all it's worth," he said. "Maybe it makes your trail more tangled than before. But you'll have to do your own figgerin'."

Chan fell silent, turning the matter over in his mind, but making no sense out of the things Billy Wing had told him.

When they loped into Rawson just as the moon faded, they passed the decrepit, sagging-roofed shack on the town's outskirts where Whiskey Jenny lived, the place dark and silent, no sign of life about it. But the hitch rail before the Spur Wheel held horses enough, and the light splashing from its expanse of windows laid a yellow smear across the boardwalks. Tying their horses to the hitchrail, Chan and Billy Wing barged through the batwings and into the saloon.

The place was packed, but the pasty-faced piano player saw the two Lazy-L men first and leaned upon a note too long, a discordant signal that swung a big-bodied, flat-faced man away from the crowded bar. This was Jube Cazborg, hired gun-hand of Caesar Rondeen, a man of mixed blood whose black, stringy hair fell below his flat-topped sombrero to form a greasy mat against his swarthy forehead. Doc Menafee was nowhere to be seen, and neither was the man both gunhands called master. But a hushed expectancy fell upon the room, and that throbbing stillness told Chan that those who made this place their head-

23

quarters were more than primed for trouble tonight.

Yet, after his first sweeping glance had read the sign, Chan crossed the room as easily as he might have moved through the Lazy-L bunkhouse, pausing before a table where a garishly-dressed youngster sat slumped, his dark, curly head pillowed in his arms.

"Mitch!" Chan said, a vast disgust in his eyes as he shook his foster-brother. "Mitch, wake up!"

Mitchell Loring took his own time complying, his eyes still blank and unsteady after he'd opened them. He was about Chan's own build, tall and lean and blue-eyed as well, but Mitch's features were more regular, and he had more than his share of good looks.

" 'Lo, Chan," he managed to mutter, and then his eyes widened as full comprehension came to him. "Sho . . . so you come back to good, ol' Texash, eh? Lookee, folksh, here's Chan Loring come home all the way from Montana. Thish calls for celebration. Yippee!"

"Get out of here, Mitch," Chan said between his teeth. "Get home, savvy. Billy, boost him into his saddle if he's too drunk to make it alone."

Mitch managed to get to his feet, weaving unsteadily, a scowl wedging itself between his brows, while antagonism stood naked in his

24

eyes. "Now jush a minute!" he muttered angrily. "Who you shink — think you're orderin' around? Same ol' Chan, huh. Playin' nursemaid for me. Just because you been up to Montana on spechial secret business for King Loring, you think you're a curly wolf, huh? Shucks, you ain't the only ranny'sh ever been beyond the Red River. I —"

Jube Cazborg came across the room, moving soundlessly for a man of his bulk, but not so soundlessly as to surprise Chan.

"Leave him alone, Loring," Cazborg said. "He didn't ask you to come after him."

Here was a man looking for an excuse to turn loose his guns, and any excuse would do. Yet, knowing that, Chan moved his left arm sidewards, his crooked elbow catching Cazborg hard in the chest, sending him a step backward.

"King Loring's dead, Mitch." Chan said, paying no heed to the gunman. "Do you hear me? Now get out to the Lazy-L where you belong."

For a moment, the jaw of Mitch Loring hung slack as he wavered on his feet, visibly shocked, and a great deal more sober than he'd been. "The King — dead," he choked, and stumbled toward the door.

Chan gave Cazborg his attention then, looking into the man's blazing eyes. "Where's

Rondeen?" Chan asked.

"Upstairs in his office, if it's anything to you." Cazborg snapped. "We've been expecting some of you Lazy-L gents, savvy. But what happened to King Loring tonight was man-to-man, mister. That don't mean that the boss is gonna be bothered by every Lazy-L ranny with a chip on his shoulder from here on out. I don't reckon Caesar Rondeen wants to waste any of his time on you. Now, git outa here and keep out — and that goes for the rest of your Lazy-L."

It was on the tip of Chan's tongue to retort that *one* Lazy-L man, at least, seemed to be welcome at the Spur Wheel, for most of Mitch Loring's spending money crossed the bar and gaming tables of this place. But suddenly he sensed the futility of any words, knowing there was only one language this man would understand. And because his promise to King Loring had made no mention of Rondeen's hirelings, Chan's fist lashed out, thudding against Cazborg's massive jaw, and spilling the man backwards to smash a chair to kindling as he went down.

At such a moment, anything might have happened. Cazborg was still conscious as he sprawled upon the floor. Both of the saloon's bartenders had dropped their hands below the mahogany, where hideout guns were kept, and the crowd was making a concerted movement to put itself out of any line of fire. But Billy Wing had a weapon in his hand, and it wavered gently in an all-embracing arc.

"I'll try and entertain the folks here, Chan," he said, and sent a stream of tobacco-juice at Cazborg's boot toe. "Yuh just lope upstairs and pay yore respects to the big auger — or whatever it is yuh've got on yore mind."

Nodding, Chan crossed to the stairs, climbing it to the hallway above and heading for the door which he knew led to Rondeen's private office, the beat of his boot heels a thunderous thing in the breathless silence. A reckless anger still seething through him, he kicked Rondeen's door open and stepped inside. The office was ornately furnished, plush drapes falling from the ceiling to mask all four walls, the color of them soft and subdued in the glow of a kerosene lamp hanging over the desk where Caesar Rondeen was seated.

"Howdy," Chan said easily, and took a moment to enjoy the man's astonishment. "Don't look so damned surprised. It's me, Chan Loring, all right. And I reckon you know what brings me here."

Chapter Three

Even as he spoke, it came to Chan that he'd voiced a challenge with a far more sinister implication than he'd intended, and for the space of a heartbeat he was cold with the consciousness that he might have no choice but to match smoke with the man he faced. But Caesar Rondeen, recovering from his first astonishment, merely smiled.

"Welcome home, Chan. I'd expected at least one Lazy-L hand would display his loyalty by coming here tonight with fire in his eye, but I didn't know you'd gotten back. Come in and speak your piece."

Against the exotic background of his office's furnishings, Caesar Rondeen made an incongruous figure, a Puritan in a pagan palace, a long, lean man in rusty black alpaca. At first glance he might have been mistaken for a circuit-riding preacher or an underfed schoolmaster, for there was something scholarly about his bony features, his sweep of salt-and-pepper hair brushed carefully back from his high forehead. But there was evil in that face as well, the empty eye socket serving to accentuate it. Gazing at him, Chan knew that here was a foe worthy of any man's steel.

"I'll speak my piece," Chan snapped, taking a step into the room. "King Loring died tonight, Rondeen. I talked to him before he died, and I know you burned him down. Probably you gave him a chance at his gun — he didn't say. That makes no never mind. The point is that you'll shortly find out the Lazy-L is moving north, heading for Montana. I've come to tell you to keep out of our way. Try stopping our drive and you'll wish you'd never heard of a Loring."

"So?" Rondeen said, pressing his finger tips together, and smiling benignly. "You're letting me in on the great secret, since it will soon be common knowledge that the Lazy-L is moving to Montana. Twenty years I've waited to topple King Loring off his throne. Do you think I've set here all this time, blind to his doings? Do you think I didn't guess why he sent you north? I have friends along the trail, boy. I could tell you the date you first looked upon Whispering Basin, and the date you turned your back to it. You got a beef contract at Fort Faraday, didn't you? Would you like me to repeat the details of it — the number of cattle you're to furnish, the price, the date set for delivery?"

Chan's widening eyes betrayed his surprise.

"You sneaking spy," he rasped, his hand instinctively brushing the cedar-handled forty-five at his hip.

"Don't do it," Rondeen advised him. "Not if you want to go on living. As a gambler, I've always found it expedient to have an extra ace or two handy. Look behind you!"

A half-turn of Chan's head gave him a glimpse of the man behind the door who leaned against the wall, a gun held carelessly in his hand. Akin to Jube Cazborg in viciousness, Doc Menafee was the exact opposite of the other gunnie in physical appearance. Built along the lines of his master, he was a tall, stringy creature with yellowish teeth and a wisp of a moustache.

"Howdy," he grinned.

"You see, you'd be dead now if I'd wished it," Rondeen went on. "But I don't wish it. Sit down, Chan. I've heard you out; now it's your turn to listen, and there's a lot I'd like to tell you. It strikes me that you and I could do a nice stroke of business together."

"Business," Chan echoed angrily. "A deal with you? If you think that yonder kill-crazy wolf could scare me that much —"

"Not at all, boy, not at all," Rondeen said in a mollifying tone. "You come from a breed that doesn't scare easily. Menafee is merely hanging around to see that you don't become

30

— er — impulsive before I finish. I'd hoped to have a little palaver with you one of these days. And now you've very thoughtfully provided the opportunity."

"I come to speak a piece," Chan retorted. "I've spoke it; and I'm not interested in anything you've got to say. You might as well get that straight."

The black-garbed man waved his words aside as a man might clear the air of cigarette smoke. "Twenty-odd years ago, Boone Loring put a bullet into my brother, Slade Rondeen," he went on. "Not long after that, he shot an eye out of me. Do you think such a debt could be wiped out in a minute? King Loring is dead, and I'm truly sorry that he is. You're surprised, Chan?"

"Tonight I trailed the King toward the Lazy-L in order to tell him I knew all his plans, to taunt him by saying that my hour to strike had come, and that I was prepared to block him at every turn. He made the mistake of going for his gun. That other time, long ago, he was lucky — tonight the aces were mine. But I'd rather that King Loring had lived so I could see him humbled in the dust. Death is kinder than some things to a man of pride. *Easy, Chan.*"

For Chan's hand had moved again, and the gun dangling from Menafee's fingers had gone rigid. With an angry shrug, Chan perched himself on the edge of a nearby chair.

"Texas holds nothing more for me," Rondeen continued. "I've grown weary of an existence that reeks of cigar smoke and stale beer. In short, I'm thinking of retiring from my present business. I'm going to belong to the landed gentry, Chan. Do you think I'd fit into the role of boss of Whispering Basin? Because that's exactly what I intend to be. You stole a march on me by filing on Whispering before my friends in the north could do it for me by proxy. But I'll find a way to beat your claim, and I'll handle old Angus McQuade if he persists in squatting there."

"When a man grows so big that he can't see his feet," Chan observed, "that's when he's likely to stumble."

Rondeen arched his brows. "A rare piece of philosophy for a saddle-whacker, Chan; but I think I can convince you of the falsity of it in my case. Was Mitch downstairs when you came into the Spur Wheel? He's going to hell fast, Mitch is, and seeing how I hate anything bearing the name of Loring, it's been a pleasure to watch him. How it must have eaten at King Loring's guts to see his boy patronizing my place, even calling me friend. But considering what a mess Mitch has made of himself, I shouldn't be surprised if King

Loring had asked *you* to point the Lazy-L north. Right?"

"What difference does that make?"

"This much," said Caesar Rondeen. "Somewhere along the trail, the Lazy-L herd might vanish. With your help, that could be arranged easily enough. Afterwards the brands could be worked over. As boss of Whispering Basin, I'll need cattle to stock my range."

Chan came to his feet so quickly as to spill his chair, his eyes blazing, the gun at his back almost forgotten.

"Rondeen, either you're drunk or you're loco," he said. "I didn't come here to make a gun-play against you. The reason I'm not starting any smoke is something you ain't going to know. But I've told you what'll happen if you interfere with the Lazy-L's drive. Do you actually think for one minute that I'll listen to any scheme to double-cross my own brand? Mister, for pure gall you take top money!"

Caesar Rondeen smiled. "How did King Loring instill that kind of loyalty in you?" he asked. "It's amazing, positively amazing. Now take Doc Menafee, here. I pay him fighting wages, and he'd do anything I ordered without asking questions about it. But somebody else could hire him away from me in a minute by offering ten dollars a month more than I'm paying him. The same holds true of Jube. Isn't that right, Doc?"

Doc Menafee made no reply, shifting his weight from one foot to the other, patently not knowing whether he was supposed to grin or growl at such a question.

"You see, it's priceless, such loyalty," Rondeen continued, obviously enjoying himself. "Tell me, Chan, how did King Loring do it?"

"You wouldn't savvy," Chan said scornfully. "You wouldn't begin to savvy a gent like King Loring."

"You're probably indebted to him for the rearing he gave you," Rondeen decided. "Oh, I know the tale of how he found you beside a burned wagon train up north, a nameless orphan he took under his wing. An imaginative cuss, the King was. For it happens that that yarn was pure fancy — hogwash in your language, Chan. Now wait a minute before you call me a liar. You were born the same day as Mitch Loring, and under the same roof. You doubt me? You were born right here in Rawson, in the house of old Doctor Turlock, who's now dead. And that was the same day that King Loring was out in the brush country putting a bullet into Slade Rondeen."

"It — it isn't so . . ." Chan said.

"No? I told you I always kept a couple of

34

extra aces handy. Here's one I've held for twenty-some years against the day when it would rake in a pot for me. So King Loring was depending on *you* to save his spread for him. You're not the nameless whelp that King Loring led you to believe you were, Chan. But you'll likely understand why he didn't dare tell you the truth. You see, you're the son of Slade Rondeen and Whiskey Jenny, his wife."

It was as though this draped room had begun to whirl, a pivoting thing with the leering face of Caesar Rondeen in the center of it, but Chan knew that churning maelstrom was within his own mind.

"You're lying," he said.

"Go ask Whiskey Jenny for the truth," Rondeen countered. "Ask her why King Loring paid her money all these years. Ah, I see you knew about that. It appears the King had something of a conscience, and he salved it by providing for the child he'd half-orphaned and the woman he'd widowed. But that doesn't change the fact that every bite of King Loring's grub you ate was charity, bestowed upon you out of pity. You still doubt me? Ask Billy Wing for the truth. I suspect he knows a great deal more than he's ever let on."

He paused, his single eye on Chan's stricken

35

face. "A bit of melodrama, eh, Chan," he purred. "You came here tonight with blood in your eye, ready to take up the Loring-Rondeen feud. And now you find that you're a Rondeen, that you've been giving your allegiance to the very man who killed your father. Do you still want your pound of flesh, *nephew?* Doc, case that hogleg of yours."

As Doc Menafee's gun slipped into leather, Rondeen spread his arms wide. "Here's your chance, Chan," he invited. "Start your smoke!"

But Chan could only stand there, his mind trying to fasten on something stable in a reeling world. Slade Rondeen had been his father. What was it the dying King Loring had wanted to know? "How do I stand with you boy?" he'd asked. One by one the pieces fitted, and because they did, Chan sensed that it was the truth Caesar Rondeen had told him, though every fiber of him wanted to cry out in denial.

"No Loring shall ever own Whispering Basin," Rondeen went on. "I'll see to that. No matter what stand you take, Chan, I'm breaking that outfit. With you to help me, it will be that much easier. No, I don't want your answer now. Just think it over, and decide for yourself whether you want to buck your own flesh and blood to help a Loring."

Turning away wordlessly, Chan stumbled

out of the office and into the hall. There'd been a little black metal box on Caesar Rondeen's desktop, he'd noticed, and now he remembered that one of the things he'd promised to do was to get that box. But nothing mattered at this moment except the need to get out into the night air, to be alone with his thoughts, to find something to hold to while his world crumbled beneath him.

Chapter Four

The son of Slade Rondeen. Not many hours ago, Chan had begged King Loring for some clue to his identity. Now he'd learned the amazing truth, and, with the knowledge, he wished he'd remained the nameless waif he'd been.

Rondeen. It was a name steeped in infamy, blackened first by one Rondeen who'd died because of his deeds, blackened anew by another who ruled here in the Spur Wheel with his marked decks and his crooked wheels and his gun-hung hirelings. And he, Chan, was also a Rondeen — the son of one, the nephew of the other.

He went downstairs like a sleepwalker, there to find Billy Wing still holding forth with his vigilant six-gun, the crowd cowering before him.

"Come on, Billy," Chan said tonelessly. "We're getting out of here."

Billy Wing backed cautiously toward the batwings, his gun still in his hand, for Jube Cazborg had come to his feet and was standing spread-legged, a thin trickle of blood running from one corner of his mouth, his eyes aflame with a fury held none too tightly in check.

"You've taken this hand," he said to Chan. "You had all the luck, but we'll meet again, younker. Mark that down in your tally book, and don't never forget it. No man lays a fist on Jube Cazborg, savvy. I'm puttin' a slug into you the first chance I get."

He'd made a dangerous, implacable enemy, had Chan, and here was the proof of it, but he looked through Jube Cazborg and beyond him, never seeing the man, and he said nothing as he followed Billy Wing out of the saloon. Even when they stepped up into their saddles, Chan held his tongue, but when they'd loped half the length of the dusty street he put out his hand, halting his companion.

"I talked to Caesar Rondeen," Chan said. "He told me more than I wanted to hear. I know who I really am, Billy. He said you could tell me whether it was the truth or not. How about it?"

For a moment Billy Wing only stared, a man bereft of speech. But his very astonishment had robbed him of his chance at denial, and he said lamely, "It was King Loring's secret, not mine, Chan. Thunder on the Pecos, I talked too damned much tonight as it was when I told you about the King payin' money to Whiskey Jenny. And I warned you that

39

you'd have to do yore own figgerin'."

"Then — it's true," Chan muttered, and saw his last hope go winging.

"I wasn't around the day the King rode into Rawson after huntin' down Slade Rondeen," Billy said. "But I can savvy what might have gone through his mind when he loped in to find his wife dead and little Mitch squallin' his head off, and another woman in the doc's house with a kid who'd never know his daddy because of what the King had did. Something like that must 'a' shore ate at the King's heart, Chan. Jenny moved outa Rawson when you weren't more'n a month old, but the King managed to find out where she'd gone. He took me along when we headed to Amarillo to find her."

"You mean the King went to get *me?*"

Billy nodded. "Whiskey Jenny wouldn't give you up at first. They's no use of me tryin' to make you believe she ever amounted to much, boy, and Gawd forgive me for speakin' of your mother that way. But at least she had a mother's heart, and she didn't aim to part with you. But the King pointed out that he could give yuh a real good raisin'. He had it figgered that Jenny didn't have no part in the doin's of Slade Rondeen, and it shore as hell followed that you weren't responsible for your daddy. So the King made his bargain.

He was to keep you and pay Jenny ever so often so's she'd never be in want. Most of the money he give her went for likker, but that weren't the King's fault."

"Then that story about a burned wagon train up in Comanche country — ?"

"Was somethin' the King invented when him and me lugged you back to the Lazy-L, Chan. The name of Rondeen was bad medicine in these parts. He wanted to spare your feelin's when you got older, so he made up that yarn about you bein' a waif. Caesar Rondeen must 'a' wormed the truth outa Jenny. And all these years he's waited for the right moment to spill it to you — damn his lousy carcass!"

"It doesn't much matter who told me," Chan said dully.

"The King aimed to tell you the truth tonight when he figgered he was a goner," Billy insisted. "Sittin' out there beneath the window, I could tell what was in his heart. But he thought a heap o' you, Chan, and he didn't want to die with you hatin' him. Me, I figgered you was too big for that. When I told you about him visitin' Whiskey Jenny, I thought you might go to her and get the truth. It was bound to come out sometime, and it was best that you knew, but I couldn't come right out and break my word to King Loring. If I'd knowed you was goin' to get it from Caesar Rondeen's lips, I'd'a' spilled the whole story — promise or no."

"God!" Chan cried.

Billy Wing jogged his horse. "You've got a lot of things to figger out, son," he observed. "It ain't for me to tell you what to do. But remember what the King said — 'A man is what he's shaped to be.' King Loring had the shapin' of you, and you're King Loring's kid, just like he said. Don't be forgetting that, Chan. And don't be forgetting that even when the King was dying from Caesar Rondeen's bullet, he made you promise not to match smoke with that skunk. You see, he didn't want you to burn down your own kin, even to avenge him. That's the kind of gent the King was."

Chan had put his horse into motion, too, and shortly they were on Rawson's outskirts and abreast of the dilapidated shack where Whiskey Jenny lived. A dim light burned in the structure now, and Chan reined short.

"Lope along, Billy," he said. "I'm stopping off to see her."

Billy frowned. "That's exactly what King Loring did earlier tonight," he observed. "The next time I saw him, he was falling outa his saddle. I'll hang around."

"No," Chan decided, bitterness twisting his

lips. "You're forgetting that I don't have to worry about Caesar Rondeen, like the King did. I'm a Rondeen myself, and Caesar isn't likely to kill his own kin. And don't fret about Jube Cazborg. He won't get his chance tonight. But Mitch is ahead on the trail somewhere, half-drunk, and fair game if somebody wants to collect another boring scalp. Better get after him."

Billy shrugged. "The King put you in charge tonight," he conceded. "I take your orders from here on out. Watch your back, *amigo*."

Nodding, Chan edged his horse toward the shack, and Billy Wing had become one with the darkness when the young Texan dismounted. For a long moment he hesitated before the makeshift door, his knuckles poised, an urge to flee growing upon him. Yet a man can never run from reality, so he drummed upon the door, hearing a faint stirring within and waiting a long minute until the door creaked open and the woman stood framed against the lamplight.

"I saw your light," he began lamely as he doffed his sombrero. "I'd like to talk to you. Can I step inside? You know who I am, don't you?"

He'd seen her a hundred times before, but he was seeing her now for the first time, a

43

Texas flower whose beauty had been blighted because her strength had never been equal to the struggle. Hers was a lined face, framed by straggly dark hair fast turning gray, and it came to him with a degree of surprise that she couldn't be much older than forty. Her clothes looked as though she'd slept in them, and the shack was as unkempt as its mistress, the crude furnishings strewn about, the sour odor of whiskey permeating the place.

"Yes," she said listlessly. "I know who you are. Come in, if you wish."

But when the door was closed behind him, and his shoulders were planted against it, he could find nothing to say, until finally he blurted out, "I'm Chan Loring. Maybe part of your deal with King Loring was that you'd never give sign that you knew me. That doesn't matter any more. Caesar Rondeen told me the truth tonight. I know you're my mother."

"So?" she said, no encouragement in her tone, and he began to perspire.

"It's — it's all been kinda sudden," he stammered. "I don't know what to say. King Loring matched smoke with Caesar Rondeen tonight, ma'am, and the King's dead. But I want you to know you'll still be taken care of. I'll always see to that. The Lazy-L's moving to Montana shortly, since graze is getting thin hereabouts. Reckon that'll be my home from then on, and I'll make a place for you if you want to come along. I'll send a wagon to carry your things when the drive starts . . ."

In all honesty, he had to admit to himself that he was hoping fiercely that she'd refuse the offer. She was silent for a while, the ghost of a smile finally tugging at her colorless lips.

"I'll come," she said. "Why not? One place is as good as another, and you'll see that I eat. So Caesar Rondeen finally played his ace. I knew he would, from the day he made me tell him the truth about you. He's no good, Caesar isn't. And you, Chan? You're staying with the Lazy-L now that you know the truth?"

Only then did he realize that he'd made no decision, yet his mind automatically ran in the old channels, reasoning as King Loring's kid had always reasoned, placing the Lazy-L above all things in his consideration.

"I don't know," he confessed. "I've gotta think — gotta think. I suppose I should have nothing to do with the spread now, seeing as King Loring did for my dad years back . . ."

For the first time there was a flutter of sympathy in her eyes, a token of an understanding heart, and she came to him, one hand faltering to his shoulder.

45

"It's hard for you, isn't it?" she said. "You're confused and all twisted inside. You can't shake off old loyalties in a minute and take on new ones. King Loring depended on you, didn't he?"

"It's a long trail north," Chan said, and remembered the thundering miles of it — the Nations where beef-hungry Comanches sometimes preyed upon herds — the Kansas Quarantine Line with irate grangers repelling the advance of the swarming longhorns — hell-roaring Dodge City, and the trail wolves who lurked along the dusty way from Doan's Crossing to distant Ogallala. "The King asked me to see that the Lazy-L got through. Mitch's heritage must be moved to Montana for him." Bitterness touched his lips again. "The ranch for him — the responsibility for me."

"Do it, Chan," she urged. "Take his herd up the trail for him."

"That's the way *you* want it?" he asked in surprise.

She nodded. "I hated no man so much as I hated King Loring once," she said. "I laid in Doc Turlock's house here in Rawson with you in my arms, and heard them tell what had happened to Slade. She was in the next room, King Loring's wife, with her firstborn. If she hadn't died in childbirth, I'd have found the strength to crawl to her and strangle her

46

with my own hands. I suppose there'll always be a part of me that will hate the Lorings. But the King made a bargain, and he kept it, every bit of it. I think we both owe it to him, Chan, to see that the Lazy-L gets to Montana."

"Then I'll do it," Chan said, and a weight was lifted from his shoulders. His decision had been made for him, and there was no disloyalty to either the living or the dead in it.

Both were silent then, the silence running on until it became awkward. There was nothing more to be said, he realized, and he fumbled with the door latch, wondering if he should kiss her, yet knowing it would be like kissing a stranger. He brushed his lips against her cheek — a compromise.

"I'll be going now," he said. "If there's anything you want, just let me know. It'll be a week before the drive will be starting."

Outside, he was like a man freed from prison, and he turned his cayuse toward the distant Lazy-L, all the events of the night keeping him company in memory as he made the miles unreel. The King was dead, and he, Chan, was a Rondeen, and yet his loyalty still belonged to the Lorings, and thus he was half of one and half of another, belonging wholly to neither. Growing weary of his own chaotic thoughts, he lifted his mount to a gallop, a man trying to run away from himself. The dawn was flaming in the east when he dismounted under the locust tree once again, and the ranch was awakening to a new day.

As he crossed to the ranch-house porch, Mitch's voice came to Chan from the building, a sober Mitch from the sound of him, and a very merry Mitch for one whose father lay dead in the bedroom beyond. Another voice mingled with Mitch's, a voice that stopped Chan in his tracks.

Far to the north, in Whispering Basin, old Angus McQuade held forth, and by all rights his daughter, Consuelo, should be there with him. But, amazingly, Consuelo McQuade was here, inside the Lazy-L ranch house, and there was no denying it.

Chapter Five

When King Loring had sent Chan north to
Montana many months before, the old
cattleman's orders had been simple and direct.
"This map's drawn from memory," King Loring had said, proffering a bit of paper. "It
may be plumb wrong in places, but I reckon
you can find Whispering Basin from it. Size
up that chunk o' grassland, Chan, and see how
it looks to you. If it'll do for a new home
for the Lazy-L, I want you to file on it for
us. I'll be waitin' for your report. Good luck,
boy. *Vaya con Dios.*"

So Chan had fixed his eye on the north star
and put many rivers behind him — the Brazos,
the Red, the Canadian, the Cimarron, the Arkansas, the Republican, and the Platte, until
finally he'd watered his horse from the Yellowstone, then followed the Whispering from
where it emptied into that historic stream back
into the sheltered basin.

Thus he had come to Whispering, finding
the basin to be all that King Loring had hoped,
but finding that others had come here first
— Angus McQuade and a group of friends,

Texans who'd driven their herds up from Mexico in search of a new home. But Angus McQuade and those others had overlooked one important detail in their haste to throw up buildings before the blizzards came. They'd neglected to file, so Chan had claimed the land for the Lazy-L.

He'd hated doing that. Somehow it seemed like taking an unfair advantage of these wayfarers from *manana* land, yet the King's orders had been explicit, and the King's need for this graze was great. But in his brief stay in Whispering Basin, Chan had come to admire dour, old red-bearded Angus McQuade and his fiery daughter, Consuelo, who owned the stubbornness of her Scotch father and the exotic beauty of her Castilian mother, dead these many years.

Under different circumstances, Chan might have pleased Consuelo. Certainly he'd wanted to, for when he'd first looked upon her, he'd known she was the girl he'd seen in his solitary campfires, the embodiment of his shapeless dreams. But destiny, unrelenting and ironic, had put them on opposite sides of a barrier built by the conflicting needs of two cattlemen — old men who'd nourished dreams of their own across the span of the years.

"Gringo pig!" Consuelo had cried the day Chan had departed. "You think this King Loring of yours own the world, just because he is a big man in one damn small corner of Texas. This is McQuade land, *ladron!* You keep to hell off of it. You come here with your longhorns, and you'll find grazing ground that smells of the gunsmoke!"

"Now look, darling," he'd grinned. "If we're going to quarrel like this, we might just as well be married. How about it? There was a Jesuit missionary spending a few days at Fort Faraday when I came through. Maybe we could run him down and put him to work."

Too angry to speak, she'd unleathered the thirty-eight she always carried and put a bullet through his sombrero that had come dangerously close to creasing his scalp. But hard on the heels of her wrath, contrition had misted her eyes, and he'd had the last word.

"Believe me, I'd rather fight myself than fight you, *señorita,*" he'd said soberly. "Maybe Whispering is big enough for all of us, but that's for the King to decide. I'll be coming back one of these days, when we fetch the Lazy-L herd to Montana. And I'll be seeing you again."

And now he was facing Consuelo McQuade once more, for she was here in the Lazy-L ranch-house living room, wearing the pleated riding skirt and full-sleeved blouse and spurred boots she'd worn when he'd seen her last. But even in such garb, there was something about the full-lipped, dark-eyed beauty of her to remind a man of that lazy land below the Rio, and to make him think of grilled casements and white lace and muted guitars in the moonlight — all the glamor of old Spain transplanted. His first astonishment passing, he knew she must have been close behind him all the way south from Montana, and he admired her because she had dared the trail alone.

"Hello darling," he grinned from the doorway. "If you'd told me you were takin' a *pasear* to Texas, it would 'a' been a pleasure to escort you."

"I passed you while you were at Fort Faraday, *señor*," she said stiffly, but he was sure her eyes had lighted at this first sight of him. "I saw you again in Ogallala and in Kansas. My business is not with you, but with King Loring. And now I'm told I come too late, that he — is *muerto* — dead."

"Chan, I figger I ought to know a little of what's going on," Mitch frowned. "From what Miss McQuade's told me since she got here an hour ago, I gather that the King sent you north to file on some land called Whispering Basin. But it seems that her people had already settled there. She claims that we're going to shove cattle north, take over the land.

52

Is that the straight of it?"

"It's a long story, Mitch, and I reckon the King would have told you soon," Chan countered. "For over twenty years your dad had his heart set on that basin, and the Lazy-L's got to find new graze, regardless. You and me have got no choice but to carry out the King's wishes and move to Whispering."

Mitch gave the girl a wry grin. "It looks like you did a lot of riding for nothing, miss," he observed. "The deal seems to be cut and dried, and no changing it."

Consuelo came out of her chair, her lips trembling. "I come here to prevent bloodshed," she said. "All of a night I argue with my father for his permission to make thees trip. Your land title will hold, *señores,* but Angus McQuade will never relinquish Whispering without the big fight. It was my hope to plead with thees King Loring of yours, to beg him to find other graze for his cattle. But I — I come too late."

"Believe me," Chan said earnestly, "I'm sorry you rode this far for an answer that can't be changed. It's no-go, Consuelo."

"Wait now, Chan," Mitch interjected soothingly. "It seems to me that the little lady has got a case. Why do we have to settle in Whispering Basin? I'm wondering who's master here now."

Chan shrugged wearily, suddenly conscious that he hadn't slept for many hours. "King Loring is still the master as far as I'm concerned," he snapped. "Whether his will changes that, I don't know. But I'll bet he left stipulations that his wish be carried out."

Temper tugged at the corners of Mitch's mouth. "We'll see," he said, and glanced at the girl. "I hope you'll be our guest as long as you're in Texas, *señorita*. And if we go north, you can ride with us. It isn't seemly that a girl should follow that trail alone."

"Am I the *niña*, a baby to be protected by big strong gringoes?" Consuelo McQuade snorted contemptuously. "I take care of myself, *señor!*"

It left very little to be said, and Chan shrugged again, bowing himself out of the room and heading for the bunkhouse, where he greeted the dozen hands of the Lazy-L for the first time since his return. Then he tumbled into the handiest bunk, to sleep like a dead man for many hours, until Billy Wing finally shook him into wakefulness.

"I let you sleep as long as I could," Billy said. "The King's to be buried inside of an hour."

There was never any great lapse of time between death and burial on the scorched Texas plains, so Chan was shortly out in the ranch-yard again, mingling with the crew and the scattering of townspeople from Rawson who'd come for King Loring's last rites.

It was late afternoon, and Mitch had busied himself in the earlier hours, arranging to have a coffin brought out from town, and engaging services of a circuit-riding preacher who'd been passing through. King Loring lay in state in the ranch house, a candle at his feet, another at his head, and there wasn't time for much more than a last look at his leathery face before the coffin was closed and carried to the grave Billy Wing had dug beside the resting place of the King's wife in the yard.

Afterwards, Chan was to remember the funeral as a dream is remembered, vague and unreal, the separate parts of the scene blurring together — grouped mourners properly solemn, the crew clutching their sombreros close to their chests, the nasal voice of the preacher, " 'I am the resurrection and the life . . .'," the thud of clods upon the coffin top.

Consuelo was still here, Chan noticed. She stood on the fringe of the crowd, her dark eyes lowered, but afterward, when the townspeople drifted away, she mounted her own saddler with a packhorse in tow, and rode toward Rawson with them. Ezra Pettigrew, the lanky lawyer from Rawson, stayed on until the crowd dispersed, beckoning to Mitch and

Chan and Billy Wing then, and leading the way back to the ranch house.

"You'll want to know about the will," the attorney said. "But it isn't to be read now. That was one of King Loring's stipulations. Gents, I rather suspect that the King guessed his days were numbered. Two weeks ago he came to me and drew up a new will. He was expecting you, Chan, back from the north, and if your report was favorable, he intended moving the Lazy-L to Montana. That job's got to be done first, gents. I'm turning the will over to Billy Wing, as the King asked. Billy can open it when the time comes."

Patently, this was not to Mitch's liking, but he made no protest. "Looks like that's the size of it," he observed with a shrug. "There's nothing to hold us here. We'll start gathering the herd first thing in the morning. Montana's a mighty long ways off."

"Whiskey Jenny will be going along with us, Mitch," Chan said. "We can rig up a wagon for her and —"

"Whiskey Jenny?" Mitch interjected. "What in hell are you talking about, Chan? You loco?"

Now was the time when the truth would have to come out, Chan decided. But he felt the eyes of Billy Wing upon him, and glanced at the old cowpoke and saw Billy vigorously shaking his head, an admonishment to silence.

"Mitch, your dad provided for Whiskey Jenny these last twenty years," Billy spoke up. "I guess he was sort of beholdin' to her since she was Slade Rondeen's widow because of the King's bullet. Afore the King died last night, he asked that she be took to Montana if she wanted to come."

For a moment Chan wondered if Mitch would guess that Billy's last statement was an outright lie, and challenge it. But Ezra Pettigrew cleared his throat. "I can verify part of that," he said. "I know that your father made sure the woman was never in want. He even mentions her in his will. You'd better let her come along, Mitchell."

And so the matter was decided, but Chan wondered why Billy Wing had taken steps to keep the whole truth from Mitch. It was bound to come out eventually, Chan reasoned. But he respected Billy's judgment, holding his own tongue, and making a mental note to discuss the matter with the old cowpoke at the first opportunity. Opportunities, though, became rare, for the roundup began next day, and in the rush and roar of it there was little time for talk.

From the first pale flush of dawn, the riders of the Lazy-L were fanning out to comb the mesquite thickets and cedar brakes for the longhorns, a far-flung snare of horses and men that daily closed in to add to the growing herd massed near the ranch house. Dust and noise and toil had become the order of the day on the Lazy-L, and there were myriad details to be attended to. On one of these days, Chan and Mitch rode to Rawson together to order supplies for the chuck wagon, and thus Chan witnessed the first meeting between Mitch and Caesar Rondeen since the death of the King.

The black-garbed saloon owner was standing before his Spur Wheel Saloon when it happened, a tall hat cocked rakishly on his head, a toothpick dangling from his mouth, and he made no move as the pair approached. But suddenly the color faded from Mitch's handsome face, his jaw jutting angrily as he came to a halt before Rondeen.

"There was a time, Rondeen, when I called you friend," Mitch said. "I thought it was smart to buck my father's wishes by hanging around your filthy saloon. Maybe that was because I believed the Loring-Rondeen feud was old stuff, and that King Loring was a stubborn coot with a perpetual chip on his shoulder. That makes no never mind. You gunned him down, and that spelled quits between you and me. Some day I'm coming after you for that chore, mister. Do we understand each other?"

"Yes," Caesar Rondeen said, and smiled.

"I think we do, Mitch."

At such a time, a spark could set off an explosion, and Chan wondered from whence the spark would come. But Mitch brushed on and the moment was past, Chan trailing after him without so much as a glance at Rondeen, a surge of admiration for his foster-brother rising within him. Wastrel and sot though he'd been, Mitch knew where his loyalty lay, and he'd spoken his piece like a man.

Later, when Mitch had turned into the mercantile store, Chan sauntered along the street, catching a glimpse of Consuelo as she stepped from the Lone Star, Rawson's only hotel. She was still in town, then. Watching her trim figure as she walked along the street, Chan felt a twinge of pity for this girl who'd come so far only to find her cause hopeless, and his desire was to go to her. But the barrier loomed bigger than ever between them, and this wasn't the time to try and surmount it.

Shrugging, he headed in the opposite direction, losing himself in thought as he walked along, conscious of nothing around him until a voice spoke from the shadowy slot between two buildings across the way.

"Loring," Jube Cazborg called softly. *"I'm dealing this hand."*

Chan fell sidewards then, slapping leather as he went down, and snapping a shot just as Jube Cazborg's gun roared. The bullet droned over Chan's head, singing a strident song, and he wondered if he'd hear the next one. But Cazborg was staggering into the street, his gun shot from his hand, his fingers limp and bloody.

"Damn you," he said, his swarthy face knotted in pain, and repeated himself monotonously. "Damn you! Damn you! Damn you!"

"Maybe you figger I was lucky just now," Chan said coldly. "Maybe I was. But you were lucky too — lucky my bullet didn't split your skull. Next time it will!"

He stood watching while Cazborg hurried down the street to the doctor's, and the startled faces that had poked from doorways disappeared again. Twice now he'd come up against this man, and twice he'd come through unscathed. But he wondered when the third time would be, and who would emerge victorious when the gun smoke settled.

It would seem, Chan judged, that even a kinship to Caesar Rondeen was no protection against the hatred of the man's hireling. Or had Rondeen sanctioned such a play, realizing that Chan had chosen to remain a Loring? Chan didn't know. When he went down the street again, Caesar Rondeen was still standing before his saloon, but now he was bareheaded, his hat beneath his arm, for he was speaking to Consuelo McQuade. He could be almighty affable when the occasion required, could Rondeen, and he was playing the gentleman to perfection.

Yet even as Chan felt a surge of resentment, it came to him that yonder couple had something in common, for each wanted to keep the Lazy-L from reaching Whispering. Stranger alliances had been made. For twenty years the storm clouds had been gathering, Chan reflected. Somewhere between the Red and the Yellowstone, the full fury of them was bound to break.

Chapter Six

Out of dust and toil and chaos had come the building of the herd, the seven days that marched in swift succession each seeing more longhorns hazed out of the chaparral and to the bedding ground, where branding fires sent their smoke spiraling upward. Heat and smoke and dust and sweat — bawling calves and sizzling branding irons — gay shouts and grim curses — rattling horns and milling hoofs — all these things endured from dawn to dusk, and the trail herd was gathered.

Cattle were here that bore King Loring's brand, but some wore Chan's private mark, and some belonged to Mitch, gifts from the King who could understand a youngster's pride in possession. And each of the Lazy-L hands owned a few heads of his own, the descendants of mossyhorns combed out of the brush in the post-war years when a million mavericks had roamed Texas, wild and free as the land that sustained them. There had been days when a man could make a start for himself by spending his free hours combing the mesquite thickets for unclaimed, unbranded mavericks, and the King had encouraged such ambitions, letting his crews' cattle graze with his own.

Now all the beef was pooled in one vast herd, a seething sea of clacking horns and bony backs, a tossing turbulence held in check by men on horseback. And upon all of them a new brand was affixed, the road brand, the insignia that would mark them as a single herd upon the trail, a triangle formed by the simple expedient of running another straight line from one point of the Lazy-L to the other in the case of King Loring's cattle, and by more devious means when the brands required drastic alteration.

"Rondeen's got friends along the trail," Chan told Mitch and Billy Wing. "He came right out and admitted that he knew every move I made when I went north. They'll be watchin' for the Lazy-L, those wolves of his. But they'll do a heap of looking without finding this Triangle herd!"

So, the herd was prepared for the trail — the younger beef that would mature in Montana, the four-year-olds consigned to Fort Faraday, the she-stuff which would make breeders when the Lazy-L re-located. Only the culls were turned back upon the range.

Guns were cleaned, and saddle gear was overhauled. Broken wagons had been mended, and the chuck wagon had long since been loaded by Stew Bidwell, cantankerous master of pots and pans, and under the canvas top had gone sugar, beans, coffee, flour, cornmeal, a keg of molasses, and a barrel of pickles, and sundry other articles designed to keep a hungry cowhand happy. Another wagon had been provided for Jenny Rondeen, who was fetched out to the Lazy-L on the eve of the drive.

"You'll have to handle the reins yourself," Chan told her. "I can't spare a man away from the herd, but if the going gets too hard, just let me know." Pausing, he'd eyed her reflectively. "I'm making no rules for the trail as far as you're concerned. But it would please me mightily if you'd tote no whiskey along."

"I understand," she said, and smiled at him enigmatically, a gesture that promised neither obedience nor defiance, and he did not press the matter.

Then there came the morning when Chan prepared to leave the ranch house for the last time, but though the drive would start at once, he lingered, inventing a dozen little chores to do and giving overly-detailed orders to the squaw housekeeper who would remain behind. In the ranch yard he tarried, too, looking long and intently at each familiar thing, building a bulwark of memory strong enough to withstand the battering of new days and ways, hesitating beside the King's grave in a silent farewell, then finally swinging into his saddle with never a backward glance.

The herd, four thousand longhorns shapeless in the spreading dawn, was already being moved to the ranch's north fence, there to be sent streaming through a gate, while the sheriff from Rawson tallied the beef and afterwards collected the customary five cents a head for the clearance papers which registered the new Triangle brand and also certified that the animals were healthy.

"What name goes on these papers?" the lawman wanted to know. "Which one of you Lorings is trail boss?"

"I am," Chan said.

And thus declaring himself, he felt the impact of Mitch's stare as though it were something tangible, but Mitch held his tongue until the sheriff had shaken hands all around and taken himself off toward Rawson. But with Chan thoughtfully stowing the clearance papers into his wallet, Mitch came down from his saddle and strode toward Chan, his movements the carefully mechanical ones of a man with things upon his mind, his hostility all too apparent.

"What am I on this spread, Chan?" he asked. "The cook's flunky?"

Irritation narrowed Chan's eyes, but his voice betrayed no feeling. "The King told me to take the outfit north," he said. "That was his last order before he died, and I'm carrying it out. If you doubt my word, Billy Wing will tell you what the King said. There's damn little glory in being a trail boss, Mitch. I didn't ask for it."

"I savvy," Mitch said angrily. "One of King Loring's kids is a drunken tramp, unfit to do a man's work. But the other is a rock that no storm can budge. The King wanted the best man for the job, so he picked you, eh? But supposing the King was wrong about which of us is the best man?"

"You must have liquor under your belt," Chan countered. "You wouldn't be talking that way otherwise, Mitch."

"I took my last drink the night the King died," Mitch snapped. "And if you think I'm talking to hear myself, climb down off that cayuse and find out!"

Chan shrugged. "What good would that do? Each of us would probably lose a few teeth and collect an eye that would need one of Stew Bidwell's beefsteaks slapped onto it. Get on your horse, Mitch, and quit behavin' like a spanked kid. We've got a trail drive to start."

"Chan, I've thought you were too good to be true," Mitch said. "I've thought a lot of

66

things about you a lot of times, but up till now I never figgered you had a yellow streak. What good would a fracas do, eh? It would decide who's boss. What the King's will has to say, I don't know, and I reckon I won't know till we hit this Whispering you talk about. But meantime, if I'm a better man than you, I've got the right to be trail boss. If you're wider across the britches than I think, I'll take your damn orders like any other hand. But there's just one way to find out!"

"No argument about that," Chan admitted, and slipped to the ground.

For it had come to him that there was no course but to accept the challenge. Since the day of the King's funeral, Mitch had grown more sullen, resenting each show of authority Chan had had to make, and letting his resentment manifest itself in many ways. Yet the real trouble between the two of them went deeper than that. This was merely the culmination of a conflict that had smouldered for a long time, the outgrowth of half-forgotten boyish squabbles. Always Chan had known that there had to be a day when one of them would prove himself master. That day had come.

Yet with a challenge made and a challenge accepted, there was no heart in Chan for the chore he must do. Always he'd felt immeasurably older than Mitch, and always his role had unconsciously been a big brother's. Often enough he'd stood between Mitch's misdeeds and the just wrath of the King. And thus each step in the relationship of these two who were brothers without a blood tie had been a step toward the ultimate showdown that had to come. Now it was here.

"Ready?" Mitch asked, and exploded into action.

He came as a longhorn charges at an unhorsed rider, head down, eyes blazing, and Chan found it no trick at all to step aside. He might have smashed Mitch down as Mitch hurtled past him, but some part of Chan demanded that Mitch must strike the first blow. And Mitch obliged him readily enough, stopping abruptly, spinning on his heel and launching a wave of fists that beat futilely upon Chan's raised guard.

Yet a blow was bound to get through, and one did, sending Chan reeling. Down upon his knees, he shook his head to free himself of the drugging effect of Mitch's fist, coming erect in time to dodge a new barrage of bunched knuckles, but finding himself hard put to hold his own.

Somewhere Mitch had gained a skill that Chan hadn't guessed his foster-brother possessed, and now to Chan this was no longer a matter of winning with the least possible damage to his adversary. Dissipation had softened Mitch, but he might have grown a dozen extra arms, and they were everywhere, pistoning fists taking such a terrific toll that Chan marshaled all his efforts to meet the threat of them.

And thereupon the tide of the battle began to turn, for with Chan giving himself wholeheartedly to the fray, all the flash and nimble-footedness went out of it, and it became a ruthless slugging match, the pair of them toe to toe, trading blows. Here the advantage was Chan's, for his was the greater power, and he put all of it behind his fists, hammering Mitch relentlessly until the fear of defeat became a betraying flame in Mitch's eyes.

But a challenger's pride still belonged to Mitch, for the man who asks for a fight suffers a double defeat when he goes down. Perhaps that is why Mitch dipped deep into his bag of tricks, feinting and weaving and making holes in Chan's guard.

Finish this soon was Chan's compelling thought, and it was repeating itself when he felt Mitch's fists explode against his jaw. The land upreared wildly, and for a moment Chan was shaken by the crazy fear that all creation had gone cattawampus, and that the longhorn herd was going to come sliding down the unstable, tilting world to crush the pair of them.

If Mitch had followed up his advantage, the fight would have been over then and there. As it was, it lasted a moment longer, and that moment was Chan's. Mitch stood spread-legged, panting and sobbing, drawing in his breath in gusty gasps. Mitch had drawn beyond his reserve of strength to accomplish his coup, and the certainty of that conviction gave Chan the strength to rise to an opportunity.

Bounding to his feet, he found himself confronted by a dozen wavering Mitches, but he hurled his fists at one, and all of them went down. Then, as Chan shook his throbbing head, he saw Mitch sprawled upon the ground, his mouth a smear of scarlet.

"Get up!" Chan croaked. "Get up and fight!"

"I — I can't," Mitch gasped, and turned over on his face, spread-eagling himself against the earth.

It would be a very simple thing, Chan decided groggily, to fall down beside Mitch, and only his will kept him on his feet. He gazed at the ring of faces around him, the solemn, wooden faces of the Lazy-L crew. In the wavering distance, Stew Bidwell, perched upon his chuck wagon, was shouting something incoherent, and farther away, Whiskey Jenny

70

leaned breathlessly forward from her wagon seat.

She was too far away for Chan to judge just what it had done to her to see a Loring and a Rondeen pitted against each other once again, but that didn't concern him. In the faces of the crew was open respect for both victor and vanquished, but a judgment was also there. *This man is master,* the look of them said, and across the miles of the thundering trail they would abide by the decision thus rendered.

"Load Mitch into Jenny Rondeen's wagon," Chan said, walking toward his horse and fighting to keep his footsteps steady. "Leave him ride there till he's able to sit a saddle. And you, Billy; get those longhorns pointed north. Me, I've got a last chore to do in Texas. I'll catch up with you long before sundown, I reckon."

Then he hauled himself into his saddle and rode away, a trail boss who'd given his orders and knew they'd be obeyed. But no man is his own master so long as a promise binds him to another man's will, and there was this one thing Chan Loring must do before he put Texas behind him.

Thus he came across the miles to Rawson once again, the sun climbing steadily above him all the while, until it stood at zenith as he walked his horse down the street to the Spur Wheel Saloon. And here Chan paused, sitting his saddle and knowing there was no use in alighting, for the Spur Wheel stood shadowy and silent, new boards nailed tightly across its windows, an air of desertion clinging to the place like a musty mantle.

He was gazing upon this change and wondering what it portended when the sheriff, an astonished lawman, hailed him from the boardwalk.

"You here, Loring!" he exclaimed. "What's the matter? Somethin' wrong with those clearance papers? Shucks, I figgered you'd be well up the trail by now."

"Caesar Rondeen?" Chan asked. "Where is he?"

The sheriff grew even more astonished. "Why, I thought you'd heard the news, or I would have told you about it this morning. Rondeen's moved out of Rawson. Gone for good, it looks like. He tried to sell the Spur Wheel, but he couldn't get a buyer in a hurry, so he loaded the saloon's equipment into wagons and took off. Him and his whole layout — Cazborg, Menafee, and every man that drawed his pay. Damned if I know where he headed."

"And that McQuade girl from Montana way," Chan added. "The one who's been staying at the Lone Star Hotel. Is she gone, too?"

"Left day before yesterday."

Jigging his mount, Chan lifted his hand in a farewell salute to the law and faced north again, a feeling of frustration upon him until he shrugged it away.

Caesar Rondeen was gone, and so was the little black box he possessed. Chan Loring had come to Rawson this last time to get that box by any means, even at gunpoint if necessary, to fulfill his other pledge to King Loring. Thus Chan had failed today, but the last hand hadn't been played. Somewhere to the north was Caesar Rondeen — and somewhere their trails would cross again.

Chapter Seven

Before that spring day dissolved into a flurry
of fantastic colors to the west, Chan Loring
overtook the slow-moving Lazy-L trail herd
to assume his place in point position. Long
since, the shapeless flow of longhorns had been
forced into a blunt arrowhead pointed north,
the swing men patroling the flanks of the herd,
their rope ends popping explosively as they
turned back wayward steers, the drag men
ranging across the dusty base of the arrowhead, while to the west Ollie Archer, the kid
wrangler, held the remuda. A mile behind
came the wagons, Stew Bidwell's and Jenny
Rondeen's.

Some were here who'd been up the trail before, veterans like Billy Wing and Pete Still
and Chan, who'd hazed longhorns as far north
as Dodge. Others of the Lazy-L were yet to
be initiated, younger hands whose experience
had been gleaned on short drives to the railroad. There was a difference on this long
march that they were quick to learn, for the
cattle weren't pushed. Rather, they grazed
forward, eating a continuous migratory meal,

each mouthful taking them further north.

There'd been no stop for a noon meal this day, nor would there be any other day. While Chan had been loping into Rawson at high noon, Stew Bidwell, at that same hour, had been driving his chuck wagon up ahead of the herd, there to bring a gallon of coffee to boil by the time the drive caught up with him. A hand could stop for a cup of the black brew if he had a mind to. But until darkness came, and a camp was made, and the cookfire made a red smear against the gloom, there was no meal for the hungry hands.

Even then, with a day's work behind the crew, the herd had to be bedded down, all hands milling them into a slow maelstrom by forcing the blunt arrowhead back upon itself, until at last the longhorns sagged down awkwardly, front legs first. Whereupon Holy Joe Hawkins, that dour, solemn-faced Lazy-L rider who'd earned his sobriquet because he carried a Bible in his bedroll and supplied slightly garbled quotations on any occasion, made a thoughtful observation. "There's one thing can be said for beef critters that can't be said for most humans," he said. "The long-horn always gets down on its knees before it goes to sleep."

Thus, after fourteen hours of toil, there came that only respite in the day of a trail-driver, supper time, each man lining past the end of the chuck wagon to help himself to the fare — and bringing down Stew Bidwell's wrath if he forgot to toss his eating utensils into the wrecking pan afterwards. Then there was a brief hour for talking as the men perched upon their bedrolls waiting for the nighthawking assignment, each hoping he wouldn't be given the second guard, from eleven till two, which snatched a man from the middle of his sleep.

This, then, was to be the order of the days that followed, each day putting fifteen miles behind them, the flatness of the prairie dropping into the distance, the trail meandering through low hills and out of them again, the drive so peaceful and serene as almost to banish the fears of Chan who knew that all this could not endure.

Somewhere ahead lurked Caesar Rondeen, and some day he'd strike, just as he'd threatened. And Consuelo McQuade? Had she joined forces with the archenemy of the Lorings? Chan didn't know, and he had other worries as well, for within his own outfit there might be dissension any day. Both Chan and Mitch still bore the marks of their recent fight, and there were hidden scars that went deeper, the scars that sear the soul when men pit themselves one against the other.

Yet there was this to be said for Mitch Loring — he'd made a bargain and he was keeping it, for he'd agreed to take orders obediently if the fight went against him. And Mitch was standing by his word, performing whatever tasks befell him, though sometimes reluctantly and with a studied sullenness that hinted of rebellion brewing deep within him.

Then the Brazos River was behind them, and the adventure of the first crossing, an uneventful one, belonged to the yesterdays, and the Red River was ahead, that turbulent boundary between Texas and the Indian Territory. Still the peace persisted, each day a monotonous counterpart of the one before it, with only the land changing as it slid to the southward and the herd moved on.

Under the spell of the smiling skies, Jenny Rondeen was blossoming into a new kind of woman, though the change manifested itself only in her outward appearance, for she maintained her customary morose silence, keeping to her own wagon during the evening hours and speaking to Chan only when she was spoken to. She had brought whiskey along, Chan soon discovered, for her flushed cheeks testified to occasional nipping. But Chan made no further remarks about the subject.

Anything that might provide for her comfort, he was quick to do, but such services as he rendered were automatic. She was still a stranger to him, this woman who'd borne Slade Rondeen's son. Sometimes he wondered if time would ever tumble down the barrier he sensed between them.

Yet her presence was enough to remind Chan of the thing he'd wanted to ask Billy Wing. He put his question one night when they rode the early guard, the shift that was the time-honored property of the trail boss and the older hands. "When do I tell Mitch the truth about myself?" Chan asked. "I'd have gotten it over with the day of the King's funeral when he jumped down my throat at the idea of taking Jen— my mother along. I shut up when I saw the look you gave me. What was on your mind, Billy?"

Billy Wing gazed across the shadowy expanse of the herd, and worried a bite of tobacco off a battered plug.

"The news'll keep from Mitch till we get to Montana, Chan," he said. "Remember, things has been purty stirring for Mitch, too, lately — the King passin' so suddenly — the outfit hittin' north, and all. You might say all those things are wakin' Mitch up, changin' him from a boy to a man. I reckon it'll be best if a *man* hears the story about you that he's gotta hear some day. They say cows age fast on the trail. Maybe so it's the same with two-legged critters. Wait a while, Chan."

"He's behaving himself," Chan admitted. "He claims to have quit drinking the night the King died, and I believe he means it. Billy, sometimes I think I don't know Mitch at all, in spite of the fact that I've growed up with him. I know he's done plenty of hell-raising these last few years, but I've always figgered he'd grow out of that. How'd he get along while I was up to Montana?"

Billy shrugged.

"He done plenty of ridin', Chan. Thunder on the Pecos, he got too damned thick with Caesar Rondeen, and there was weeks when the Lazy-L shore didn't see much o' Mitch. But don't you worry about that boy. He's King Loring's kid, remember, and blood's bound to tell. He'll turn out to be a top-hand yet."

Chan nodded soberly, a bow to the wisdom of this old man who'd lived much and profited by living.

"Speaking of Rondeen," Chan said, "I'm wonderin' where he's keeping himself. I told you how he hightailed out of Rawson. He don't aim that we should ever see Whispering, Billy. And he isn't likely to wait until we wet our feet in the Yellowstone before he strikes."

They'd veered westward from the regular trail, partly to find better graze, partly to

79

throw Rondeen off the scent if he was waiting ahead. Horseback news had it that trail wolves held forth at Doan's Crossing, outlaws who preyed upon drovers, striking in the night, then vanishing into the wild reaches of the Nations, to the north. But the Triangle outfit was not to see Doan's, that storied ford of the Red that had become a legend.

Now, with the Red River just ahead, the rains had come, whispering out of a sullen, overcast sky, making the longhorns maddeningly recalcitrant, turning the dust of the drag into a sea of squishy hoof-churned mud. Gone were the sunny, peaceful yesterdays. It was roll out of the blankets at the crack of a scowling dawn, snatch a cup of coffee for breakfast, take the kinks out of sharp-tempered saddlers, and get on to the Herculean task of hazing the herd. And with the weeping skies hanging a curtain across the land, they came through it to the bank of that stream dreaded most by trail men, save for the Canadian, and the crossing of the Red was about to begin.

The river was running bank-full when Chan and Billy gazed upon it, a turbulent, muddy stream, swollen by the ceaseless rains of the past few days, a churning challenge to those who had to cross it. Old Billy frowned thoughtfully as he eyed that stretch of rain-hazy water. "You gonna try it, Chan?" he asked. "Or are you gonna wait for this rain to ease off?"

"We'll try it," Chan decided after a long moment of debating. Lost days can pile upon each other, tearing a schedule to tatters, and Fort Faraday wouldn't wait forever for soldier beef. "You and me can push a few head across and see how it goes," he added. "Believe it or not, *this* was a ford when I came south from Montana!"

Nodding, Billy turned his horse to haze out a small bunch of leaders. Heading these toward the river, Chan and Billy galloped along behind the steers, hitting the water with a tremendous splash, and fighting the tugging current as they swam after the longhorns. There were times during that crossing when Chan was sure he'd be snatched off his horse, swept downstream. But at last the two men stood dripping upon the north bank, considerably to the east of the point where they'd entered the river. The test had been successful, and Chan raised his arm in a slicing gesture to the distant crew, ordering them to bring the main herd across the river.

And now they came, urged on by the crew, heads and horns freckling the turbulent flood, bellows of fear cutting above the hiss of the rain as the longhorns were prodded into the stream, churning it to a yellowish froth, their bony backs bridging the river from bank to bank as the leaders gained the north shore while the drags were still on the south side.

Forcing his horse back into the river, Chan started across to lend a hand. They'd need all the help they could get, those toiling Lazy-L riders, for already some of them were unhorsed, swimming along as best they could and clinging to their mounts' tails. Chan caught a glimpse of the pale, stricken face of Lonnie Reese, youngest of the Lazy-L crew. Lonnie's horse had vanished from sight, and the youngster was threshing wildly, blindly in the water. Veering to lend him a hand, Chan saw Pete Still, who was much closer, reach out to collar the floundering boy.

It was moment when Chan doubted his own wisdom in attempting a crossing at such a time, for here was confusion gone crazy, men and steers and horses merged into one chaotic pattern of effort and sound. And then, above all, there came a new note, ominous and unmistakable — the sharp smack of bullets striking the water.

Lifting his startled eyes, Chan peered hard, trying to pierce that sleazy wetness that changed sky and land and river into one. Yet he didn't need to see who was yonder on the south bank to realize the dread import of what they were doing. Riflemen were laying a barrage of bullets into the midst of the Lazy-L, attacking the herd and the crew at a time when they had no means of defending themselves. It was like shooting fish in a rain-barrel.

Not many nights ago Chan had been wondering when Caesar Rondeen would strike. Now he knew that Rondeen had chosen his time — chosen it wisely and well.

Chapter Eight

Somewhere in the course of his life span, a man always learns that the anticipation of danger can be more harrowing than the actuality. A shadow, having no substance, makes an elusive and awesome antagonist. Thus to Chan Loring, swimming the rain-tossed Red with bushwhack bullets pelting about him, there came a feeling that had nothing of fear in it.

Caesar Rondeen had found them out. Caesar Rondeen, probably by the simple expedient of sending scouts in many directions, had seen through the Lazy-L's subterfuge of changing brands and taking a different trail. But now that Rondeen had forced the fight upon them at last, the challenge could be met.

And Chan was going to meet it! A promise to King Loring had put Rondeen beyond the reach of Chan's powder smoke, and a knowledge that a blood tie bound him to the King's ancient foe might also have stayed his trigger finger if Chan were standing face to face with Rondeen. But there could be no turning the other cheek to a Colt, and besides, with the rushing rain throwing a veil over everything, the fight to come would be an impersonal one, blind man against blind man.

His horse staggering across the narrow strip of beach and lurching up the south bank, Chan saw that most of the herd was into the water. Stew Bidwell's wagon and Jenny Rondeen's still stood upon the bank, waiting to be taken across. The old cook, a gun in his hand, cowered hesitantly behind a wagon wheel, seeking a target where none was to be found. Afraid that his own weapon might be water-fouled, Chan snatched Bidwell's gun and drove into the storm with it.

For he'd marked the jagged ribbons of flame that cut through the drizzle, and he knew where he'd find the raiders. Yonder loomed a bluff, crowding to the very edge of the river, and upon it the foe was perched, firing blindly, apparently, choosing no targets but tossing bullets promiscuously in the general direction of the crossing, the wild bellowing of the cattle serving as a lodestone to draw their lead.

Slipping from his saddle, Chan zig-zagged forward, clambering up the slope of the bluff and pausing only long enough to lay three pistol shots so closely spaced that the roar of them blended into a single roll of sound. Above, a man cursed shrilly, and because that voice belonged to Doc Menafee, Chan lost any lingering suspicion that this might be trail wolves from Doan's Crossing, men who'd seen prime beef for the taking and seized opportunity at its ripest. Rondeen was here — and no mistake about that.

But if Chan's shot had taken some sort of toll, the blare of his gun had also served to betray his presence, so he flattened himself against the muddy ground as an answering buzz of lead droned above him. Holding his own fire, he awaited a respite in the enemy's volley, wishing heartily the while that other Lazy-L hands were here to back him against such odds.

"One of them's down there," a renegade's voice snarled, the rain making it bodiless. "I saw his gunflash. They're carrying the fight to us!"

"Sounds like most of the herd is across the river," another spoke up. "Maybe the crew's comin' back over to try and smoke us out. Wish I could see — *Damn!*"

"Down, you fools!" That was Caesar Rondeen speaking. "They've circled around us. Jube just got nicked by a rifleshot that came from the southeast."

Now there came the steady beat of rifle fire, and who ever was behind that gun was doing a thorough job of it, spacing the shots evenly and laying each one where it would leave consternation in its wake. Chan's first thought was that Stew Bidwell had dug a long gun out of his gear and had maneuvered to a flanking position to loose a load of trouble upon the enemy. But there hadn't been time for the cook to have made any such move, and the truth discounted the theory. Coming to his feet, Chan fired again.

Other forms were looming behind him in the rain, and he heard Mitch's voice and the nasal twang of Holy Joe Hawkins. The Lazy-L had turned back to side its trail boss, the riders moving forward together. But Rondeen's outfit had suddenly lost all stomach for the fight. Saddle leather was squealing upon the bluff as men hastily mounted, their voices mingling in a medley of curses and angry shouts, for still that rifle yammered yonderly. Caught in a crossfire, Rondeen chose to retreat. One rifle, Chan realized, had turned the tide of battle.

Streaming down the side of the bluff, Rondeen's outfit — a half-dozen men, Chan guessed — streaked into the rain and vanished. But still Chan charged forward, shouting to identify himself. "Lazy-L!" he cried, and the rifle went silent; and when he rounded the bluff, a figure rose from a cluster of rocks, and Chan paused, paralyzed by the sight. For it was Consuelo McQuade who'd taken the side of King Loring's men and put Rondeen to flight!

"You!" he exclaimed.

Mud made a smear against her cheek, and there was something utterly incongruous in the picture she presented, her flower-like face radiant with a smile while her slim fingers busily reloaded her smoking rifle. Mitch, swinging up beside Chan, came out of his saddle with considerable alacrity, rushing forward and seizing her hand.

"We owe you a mighty big heap of thanks," he murmured. "If you hadn't taken cards, those skunks would have kept us so busy dodging bullets that our herd would have been scattered down the Red plumb to the Gulf. *Señorita,* you sure played your cards at the right time."

"And I thought that maybe you were stringin' along with Rondeen!" Chan sighed.

"That *bandido,*" she said. "That — that *chivato*. In Rawson he make the beeg talk to me about how beautiful is his friendship in hees youth to my *padre,* Angus McQuade. We should string along together, this Caesar Rondeen and me, to see that the Lorings do not come to Whispering. But my father has told me, long time ago, that Rondeens are no good. And I tell thees one so."

Chan winced. "Just the same, I didn't figger you'd fight him to help *us* out. And I'm mighty grateful."

"My pack horse strayed, and I lost two days on the trail looking for that cayuse," she said. "That's how I come to be behind you. When this Rondeen *hombre* pass me in the storm, I hear him talk about the bushwhack trap he will make at the river. Me, I don't care for thees shootin' at men who can't shoot back. That is why I make thees gon of mine do some singing. I do the same for anybody, *señor*."

"I see." Chan grinned. "It doesn't change the fact that 'anybody' happened to be us. Back at the Lazy-L, Mitch, here, asked you to trail along with us when you headed north. Like he said, the trail's no place for a lone girl. I'm seconding that invitation, *señorita*."

Her eyes flamed scornfully. "And I tell you then that I am not the baby who needs gringoes to protect me. I ride alone, *señor!*"

Whereupon Chan made a great show of solemnity, keeping his high-boned face rigid with an effort. "The shoe's on the other foot," he said. "The idea is that my outfit would feel a heap safer if your rifle was along to side us. We'll have to be enemies when we reach Whisperin', I reckon, but meantime we've got a few common enemies ahead. A temporary truce might be a good thing all around. Beyond the Red River lies Comanche country, remember."

Which ended the argument, for Consuelo

89

said nothing, contenting herself with a contemptuous snort which might have withered the entire Comanche nation and scorched the edges of the Kiowas, the Choctaws, and kindred tribes. And with the deadlock building silently, Billy Wing, who'd re-crossed the Red also, offered a somber interruption, saying, "Chan, we've got a grave to dig."

"A grave?"

"For Lonnie Reese. The younker couldn't swim. Pete Still dragged him out of the river, but he weren't able to drag him out in time."

It took the laughter out of Chan's eyes, that news, a vivid picture coming back to him of the kid cowhand as he'd last seen Lonnie, threshing wildly in the churning water. Now Lonnie lay upon the south bank where Pete Still had fetched him, a tarp thrown over the still form.

Thus had the trail taken its first toll, and it was a grim, silent Lazy-L crew that held a funeral there on the Texas side of the Red, Holy Joe Hawkins officiating at Chan's request, reading a brief passage from his Bible and intoning a briefer prayer. Rain puddled into the open grave, and the sky scowled down as men who'd shared their blankets with Lonnie Reese now lowered him to his rest with their saddle ropes. Then the grave was filled, the funeral over, the men turning back to the tasks at hand.

The wagons had to be ferried across the river, cottonwood drift logs lashed to the sides of them, and Consuelo rode over on one, her saddler swimming behind. She mounted again on the north bank, and, once the herd was bunched and headed onward, she rode with it. Before that day was done, she was significantly perched upon the seat of Jenny Rondeen's wagon, the reins in her hands. She'd made her decision, and Chan breathed easier, knowing she'd have armed escort across the miles ahead.

For now the Triangle herd was into Indian Territory, trespassing on land belonging by treaty to the Comanches and other tribes. The rainstorm passed with the second day, but another storm might be building, more devastating than anything wrought by nature's hand. The Comanches weren't the wild raiders that they'd been a score of years before, but even though they were confined to this land that would one day be the state of Oklahoma, they were still a menace to interlopers. For the Comanches had learned that the only way to preserve their grassland for the antelope and the buffalo that sustained the redmen, was to fight against the encroaching Texans who fixed their eye on the north star and chose the most direct route to Dodge, regardless of hell, high water, or a heathen's dubious rights.

Nor had Chan forgotten that Caesar Rondeen might soon show himself again. Thus there were subtle changes in the routine of the drive. Each night young Ollie Archer kept his remuda closer to camp, and the wagons crowded the rim of the campfire where once they'd stood apart in a lonely sort of aloofness. And in the daylight hours the wagons no longer lagged a mile behind, out of the dust of the drag, but hugged the very heels of the rear-guard riders.

And so, with every move made for the mutual protection of all concerned, each man's faculties were sharpened by the sense of hovering danger, and there was no surprise the day the Comanches came.

Pete Still, riding a flank position, saw them first, his shrill shout drawing every eye to the low bluff over which a score or so of painted horsemen came streaming. Wheeling his own horse, Chan gave the signal to mill the herd, and helped in the task, then rode swiftly back toward the rear, Billy Wing quirting beside him, the other riders also thundering along toward the wagons which had come to a bone-jolting halt. And there, in a circle around the canvas-tops, the bulk of the Lazy-L crew reined short, sitting their saddles and presenting a formidable front to the oncoming redskins.

"A sizeable party," Billy commented. "Thunder on the Pecos, Chan, they've got us outnumbered. But likely they'll make no trouble if we don't."

"I'm not so sure," Chan said, and his lips fashioned themselves into a straight line, eloquent of his grim fears. "If I'm not reading the sign wrong, that bunch is full of firewater to the eyebrows. A drunken Indian usually isn't in a reasonin' mood."

"To hell with them!" Mitch said, his dark, handsome face betraying all of a Texan's loathing for a redskin, a culminating heritage of hatred bred of fifty years of frontier warfare, so bitter that Texas, of all the border states, was the only one which never had a squaw man in its history.

"Watch yourself, Mitch." Chan retorted. "You draw a gun and we'll likely all part with our scalps. Those devils aren't packin' bows and arrows. They've got repeating rifles, you'll notice. Our only cue is to outbluff 'em. Crack a cap and there'll be out-and-out war."

The Comanches had drawn to a halt not many yards away, a half-naked group, their cheeks daubed with paint. Most of them were young bucks, and most of them were drunk, but their leader was older than the rest and comparatively sober. No feathered war bonnet marked him for what he was, for his badge of leadership was in his bearing. To him Billy Wing spoke in the Comanche tongue, listening in return to a long harangue which the old man finally translated to Chan.

"Our *amigo,* Rondeen, has showed his hand again," Billy scowled. "He's their 'very good friend,' accordin' to them. Seems he gave 'em whiskey and told 'em we were coming here to make big trouble for them. I've told the chief that Rondeen talked with a forked tongue, that we're just passin' through and don't aim on harmin' anybody."

"Think you convinced him?" Chan asked.

"The chief's no fool," Billy observed. "He knows he could wipe out the bunch o' us, but there'd be a few good Injuns made outa bad uns afore the fracas was over. Rondeen didn't pour quite enough whiskey into him. But them bucks of his'n may get out of hand. Take a look at that one!"

A young Comanche had slipped from his horse. Naked from the waist up, he was lean as a panther, a splendid figure. But whiskey had rendered his legs unsteady, and he staggered forward between the Lazy-L riders, lurching toward the chuck wagon and peering inside, Stew Bidwell suffering this indignity in stony silence.

At this moment an electrified hush fell upon both groups, the red and the white, every man tense with the realization that a false move on anybody's part might precipitate a general melee. Climbing into the chuck wagon, the young Comanche soon lurched into view again, clutching a partially-filled flour sack. Grasping it by its bottom, he spun the sack about his head, laughing uproariously as flour streamed everywhere.

"If they think they can scatter our grub — !" Mitch began angrily, but Chan's sharp glance quieted him.

The flour sack empty, the Comanche was looking for a new source of amusement, his eyes roving everywhere and lighting at last upon Consuelo who sat stiffly erect on the seat of Jenny Rondeen's wagon. Just for an instant the Indian hesitated. Then his eyes alight with some new devilishness, he reeled toward the girl.

Everything happened at once then. The Comanche chief barked a low, guttural order, emphatic enough to stop the buck in his tracks. But Chan was already moving forward, and so was Mitch — the difference being that Mitch was reaching for his gun. The crisis had been reached and passed, that single order of the chief's turning the tide, for the older Indian had seen the shape of big trouble ahead

95

and chosen to avoid it. But Mitch had his finger on the trigger, and a dead Indian would change the entire situation.

There was no time for thinking, and Chan's action was instinctive. His own gun leaped into his hand, and he laid the barrel of it alongside Mitch's head, knocking him from his saddle to the ground, where he sprawled, half-stunned and bleeding. At the same time the Comanche chief lifted his arm in a swooping signal, and his braves wheeled their mounts, galloping away, the young buck catching his horse on the fly, swinging astride it with an effortless motion in spite of his drunkenness.

Thus the danger passed, but Mitch, reeling to his feet, was in no mood for jubilation. "You — you pistol-whipped me." he snarled at Chan. "You used a gun on me in front of the whole crew and a passel of lousy Indians."

"You damn fool!" Billy Wing snorted. "He saved your life and the skin of every one of us. If you'd plugged that buck after his chief had ordered him to lay off his deviltry, there'd been hell turned loose."

"I don't give a damn!" Mitch spat. "I'm not forgettin' this deal. I don't think that the King forgot his own flesh and blood when he made out his will. And the first chore I'm doing when I'm legally the boss of the Lazy-L

96

is to give you walking papers, Chan. Just remember that. You're through the day I've got the power to boot you out."

Chapter Nine

Their old antagonism had fanned into flame, and even though Mitch Loring spoke in the heat of that flame, he'd meant what he said, and he'd remember his own threat long after the passion that prompted it had gone out of him. Of that, Chan was sure.

Some were here who understood all too well what Chan's act had averted, older hands who'd brushed with Comanches before. Billy Wing, alone, had spoken in Chan's defense, the other riders sitting woodenfaced, withholding their judgment. But Consuelo's dark eyes held a look of reproach, and there was horror in the face of Jenny Rondeen as she gazed at Mitch, seeing the bloody havoc Chan's gun barrel had wrought.

"All right, Mitch," Chan said quietly. "Your grudge will keep until we reach Whispering. Come on, boys; let's get this herd moving."

For that was the way of cattleland on the march; the herd came first, and the herd must go on, all other things being secondary and relegated to that distant rendezvous — trail's end. But with the cattle moving, Chan left the point position to Billy, saying, "Me, I'm takin' a little *pasear* on my lonesome, pard. I'd like to have a look at the man who feeds whiskey to redskins and turns them loose on Texans and women."

"You be careful," was Billy's only admonishment, and Chan wondered what sternness in his own face had checked any argument Billy might have made against so foolish a move as a lone scouting trip in Indian country.

Angling away from the arrowhead of cattle, Chan followed the spoor of the vanished Comanches, knowing it would lead him to Caesar Rondeen, but having no idea what he'd do when he found the man. He'd put a low divide between himself and the herd, and was following the cottonwood forest that fringed a nameless creek, before it came to him that his altercation with Mitch had given him a gnawing need for action of some sort — a means to give vent to his simmering anger. Chan Loring was a man spoiling for a fight, and he rode rashly now in search of one.

Yet there was more to it than that. Since the night in the Spur Wheel Saloon when Caesar Rondeen had played his twenty-year-old ace, revealing Chan's identity to him, Chan had searched his own soul in vain, seeking the place where his allegiance lay. Somehow he had to settle the matter for once and for all, and his hunch was that his decision would be made when he faced Caesar Rondeen.

Rondeen was his kin, and therefore he, Chan, had recoiled from pitting himself personally against the man. Until today. But Rondeen had sprung a bushwhack trap on the bank of the Red, and a Lazy-L hand had died in the river. And Rondeen had struck again today, indirectly of course, but with fiendish savagery. Sooner or later Chan must accept the persistent challenge of the man, either by declaring open warfare against Rondeen, or by fading out of the fight, leaving it to men like Billy Wing, who had no personal stake in the issue.

And so he came indecisively across the miles, until the barking of dogs drew him to his ultimate destination, the camp of the Comanches, here on the creek bank. Yonder it lay, partly visible through the canopy of crowding branches, a semi-circle of buffalo-hide lodges.

Wagons were here as well — heaped, canvas-topped wagons — and by such a token Chan knew that Caesar Rondeen and his crew were in the Indian camp. And now Chan shaped a purpose out of his rashness. At least he might be able to learn something of Rondeen's plans, if luck favored him and he could get close enough to the renegade to overhear any talk.

Leaving his horse behind, he wormed forward on foot, testing each step before he took it, thankful that the fretful murmur of the creek covered the slight noise that he made. Finally he threw himself prone, inching into a position where he had a better view of the camp, a panorama made of a score of teepees with squaws tending cookfires before them, while naked children played about and dogs snapped at each other, snarling and bickering — a scene utterly primitive.

Rondeen had drawn his wagons inside the semi-circle, and one wagon bore a barrel of whiskey with a dripping spigot. The man himself stood prominently in the foreground, still clad in black alpaca, though trail dust had given it a grayish hue. Doc Menafee was here also, his arm in a crude sling to satisfy that Chan's shots back on the bank of the Red had indeed taken toll.

Jube Cazborg, too, wore a grimy bandage on his gun hand, a memento of that day in Rawson when his bushwhack trap had backfired on him. There were probably a dozen white men in all, certainly a greater number than had been atop the bluff on the banks of the Red. They were gathered around a haughty-faced Indian whom Chan instantly recognized as the chief of the group which had stopped the herd.

At such a distance there was no telling what was being said, but anger made its mark on Caesar Rondeen's bony features, and he was gesticulating eloquently as he spoke to Cazborg. What manner of an alliance was this, Chan wondered, that kept Rondeen safe in a Comanche camp? Whiskey wrought a certain magic, but its power was doubled-edged. The swarthy features of Jube Cazborg gave Chan a clue to the answer, and he guessed that the gun-hand's mixed blood had provided an entree for Rondeen and the rest.

And in the midst of his reasoning, a crushing weight flattened Chan against the ground, almost snatching the breath from him.

An Indian had leaped upon his back, a Comanche who'd undoubtedly detected Chan's presence here, and maneuvered behind him to launch this surprise attack. Chan had one glimpse of a scowling, coppery face, then he was arching his back, catapulting the Indian over his head. Lurching to his feet, Chan found himself with his hands full, for the Indian's strident scream was fetching others, a half-dozen redskins who came running to heap themselves upon Chan, bearing him backward by the sheer weight of numbers.

The fight was as hectic as it was short-lived, Chan hurling men to left and right, fighting with fist and boot and elbow, trying desperately to reach his guns. He was possessed of the strength of desperation, but superior numbers beat him down, the Indians snatching his six-guns away, lashing his arms behind him, nimble fingers probing through his pockets for hide-out weapons. Then he was hoisted to his feet, roughly thrust forward into the camp where Caesar Rondeen awaited him, the man standing with folded arms, smiling after recovering from his first start of surprise.

"Why hello, Chan," Rondeen beamed, and his next gesture left Chan weak with astonishment. Drawing a keen-bladed knife from his boot top, Rondeen stepped forward and sawed at the bonds holding Chan.

"Sit down," Rondeen invited him warmly as the rawhide fell away. "I'm sure you'll overlook the rough sort of welcome you received. After all, these redskin friends of mine had no idea what purpose brought you here. But I'll very shortly explain to the chief that you're my nephew and must be accorded the proper treatment."

"I want no favors from you," Chan said. "Or from these Comanche devils of yours either."

"Ah, the same old hot-headedness," Rondeen sighed. "Slade was impetuous, too. Will you never learn, Chan, that I'm your friend as well as your kin? There is so much that we could gain together, if you'd only see eye to eye with me. And now you've provided another opportunity for us to talk things over. But King Loring still has you under his spell, eh? A truly marvelous thing, Chan. The King dies, but his power lives on."

"Now, listen — !" Chan began angrily.

"Or have you transferred your loyalty to Mitch?" Rondeen went on. "I'd find that hard to believe, since I'm told that the two of you threw fists at each other in right royal fashion the day the drive left the Lazy-L. And, prophetically enough, the Rondeen was the conqueror. Oh yes, I know all about the fight. One of my boys lingered behind to watch the direction of your departure, then overtook me to report. And today, according to what my red friends here tell me, you used a pistol on Mitch to save him from the sad consequences of his own rashness. Surely then, all is not sunshine and roses between you and the King's cub?"

"That doesn't matter!" Chan countered, and instantly knew that he'd betrayed himself into an admission that trouble had indeed flared between himself and Mitch. "Regardless of anything else, I'd still rather string along with an outfit like the Lazy-L than team with a galoot who believes in bushwhacking and sending Indians against white men and women. I can't help the blood-tie between us, Rondeen, but that doesn't mean I've got to stomach your dirty ways!"

Anger glinted in Rondeen's single eye, but he controlled himself. Striding to one of his wagons, he disappeared under the canvas top, only to reappear a few minutes later clutching an article under his arm. The sight of it narrowed Chan's eyes, for it was the black metal box which had stood upon Rondeen's desk top back in Rawson.

"You display a spark of interest, I see," Rondeen observed. "I take it, then, that you have an inkling of what this box contains. The King told you, I presume. Very well, you can appreciate its value then. To me it is an interesting trinket, an ace, perhaps, that may be played at some future date. To you it could be a lot more."

"Meanin' — ?"

"With this in your hands, you could be undisputed master of the Lazy-L, and Mitch would be — how shall we put it? — out of the picture. That would be a nice stroke of business, turning the Lazy-L into a *Rondeen* outfit. You and I could rule Whispering between us, keeping the basin sort of in the family, as it were. But the practical use of this box would require your cooperation.

What do you say?"

Chan said nothing at first, staring at that black box in the fascinated manner of a bird staring at a hovering snake. Here it was, the thing King Loring had commissioned him to get, and by a word he could have it. Yet his bargain with the King had been that the contents of the box would be destroyed without Chan examining it. Caesar Rondeen had no intention of having that happen, Chan knew.

He wanted to ask questions, to discover exactly what the box contained. Yet to ask questions would mean betraying the limitation of his own knowledge, thereby depriving himself of the only card he held. Caesar Rondeen presumed that he, Chan, knew all there was to know about that box and was, accordingly, interested in putting its contents to use. Caesar Rondeen might not be so anxious to strike a bargain, enlisting Chan's aid, if he knew how utterly in the dark Chan was.

All of which was guesswork on Chan's part, and none of it changed the fact that he must make a choice. It was throw in with Rondeen or suffer the consequences. But still the minutes marched on, the crowding Indians eyeing him curiously, Caesar Rondeen waiting with a great show of patience, Jube Cazborg favoring the prisoner with a malevolent stare, hatred naked in the gunman's eyes.

106

"And supposing I'm not interested?" Chan asked. "What then?"

Rondeen shrugged. "Must we discuss anything so unpleasant?" he countered. "You invaded this camp, remember; and with hostile intentions, for all our Indian friends, here, know. If you persist in refusing to acknowledge that our kinship has any significance, then I have little choice but to be equally cold-hearted. What's your decision, nephew?"

"There's one thing you and I don't agree upon," Chan said slowly. "And we'd differ on that point if we tried to take over Whispering together. You make war on women, and I don't want any part of that. I —"

"I see!" Rondeen cried. "Things have changed now that young Miss McQuade has favored your outfit with her charming company. She *is* the girl that the Indians saw in one of your wagons, isn't she? An exotic type, Chan, and I can readily understand her softening influence upon you. Your father favored the dark beauties, too, although to look at Whiskey Jenny now, one wouldn't think that his tastes —"

That was as far as he got. Chan hit him then, putting all his fury behind his bunched knuckles, his rising wrath so great that the consequences of such an act were no concern at the moment. And as his fist caromed off

107

Rondeen's long jaw, the man spilled backward into the arms of Cazborg, only to bound forward again, his face flaming, and the anger in his single eye was his master now.

"So you've made your choice at last," he said. "You've dared to strike *me*. Very well. Now we know exactly how we stand, Chan. You're paying for this."

"Let me have him, chief," Jube Cazberg pleaded softly, and the devil would have cringed before the unmasked savagery in the gunman's face. "Ever since we left Texas, I've dreamed of a chance like this. These Indians have a dozen ways to make a man die, but I can give 'em cards and spades and improve on any damn' method they've got. Let me have him, chief. If you owe me anything for me getting these redskins on our side, turn him over to me!"

Chapter Ten

This was a moment when Chan's first instinct was to run, but he stood his ground instead, for the futility of flight was all too apparent. Scant chance of escaping with that red ring around him, and since there could be nothing gained by such an attempt, there might at least be some slight satisfaction in facing his fate without flinching.

More than that, he had the honor of his own breed to uphold. A hundred herds might come this way before the season was over. A thousand drovers might live because one lone Texan had taught a Comanche camp that his kind of man took a lot of killing.

For he was doomed to die, and no mistake about that. His death sentence was written across Caesar Rondeen's rage-twisted face, and Jube Cazborg wasn't going to let such an opportunity slip through his fingers. The Indians themselves were the unpredictable element, but they were merely pawns in the game. This was white man's business, and they would reason that one dead drover would be one less to trespass across the grassland in the days to come.

Or so Chan thought.

But with Rondeen's crew about to lay violent hands on Chan, the Comanche chieftain walked into the closing circle, elbowing men to right and left, speaking swiftly in his own tongue. And before his barrage of words Cazborg scowled angrily, Rondeen staring blankly the while, proof enough that he understood no part of the palaver.

Touching Chan's chest, the chief gesticulated toward a distant lodge where a young buck sprawled, snoring lustily, deep in drunken sleep. Most Indians looked alike to Chan, but he knew that one. It was the young Comanche who'd begun a display of deviltry by invading the chuck wagon when the redskins had stopped the Triangle herd.

Still the point and the purpose of all this harangue remained a mystery to Chan, and obviously to Rondeen as well, for Cazborg, who was apparently the only white who understood the Comanche tongue, had no time to interpret. But when the chief turned his haughty stare upon Caesar Rondeen and spoke directly to the man, he salted his speech with a sprinkling of border Spanish, and Chan caught the one word, *"hijo."* Since *hijo* means son in the language of *mañana* land, Chan began to understand, seeing a first faint glimmer of hope.

"He says we can't harm this galoot," Cazborg translated wrathfully. "He says it was his son that Loring saved. Seems yonder buck was the one who put on a show when they stopped the herd, cavortin' around to see whether the whites scared easy. Like this redskin told us before, Mitch Loring grabbed for a gun, and he'd likely have shot the chief's son dead if this hombre here hadn't pistol-whipped Mitch. On top of that, the chief says that Loring proved he was a brave jasper by comin' to this camp alone, and the chief won't stand for no rough stuff."

"Tell him we have much whiskey and trade goods in our wagons," Rondeen said quickly. "Tell him there'll be many presents for him and his people if he doesn't interfere."

Followed a lengthy exchange in the Comanche tongue, for apparently the chief's knowledge of Spanish was too limited to sustain a full-sized conversation. Cazborg's swarthy face grew blacker as he listened.

"He says he wants no more whiskey among his people," Cazborg translated at last. "He's weary of fighting against the Texans, and says that firewater only gets his bucks into bad trouble. I tried a few arguments of my own, boss. There's no shaking him."

Caesar Rondeen instantly underwent a

marked transformation, the anger fading from his eyes and an unctuous smile spreading itself the width of his bony face. He bowed toward Chan saying, "You have a guardian angel, it seems, nephew, although his wings are noticeably missing and he smells to high heaven. Or perhaps I should make a reference to bread cast upon the waters? In any case, this aboriginal autocrat will stand for no damage to your precious hide. Regrettable, isn't it. Not only would I like to return the blow you gave me, but I rather suspect that the trail herd wouldn't get far without your able guidance. But we shall meet again, I think. And soon. Good day to you."

Taking Chan's six-guns from the Indian who held them, he presented the weapons to Chan with a flourish. But Jube Cazborg accepted the outcome of this episode with no such grace. "Your kind of luck can't last forever, Loring," he growled. "Like the boss says, we'll meet again. And next time, things is gonna be a helluva lot different!"

To each of them Chan gave a steady stare, then extended his hand white-man fashion to the Comanche chief. But the Indian chose to ignore it. Turning his back on all of them, Chan strode from the camp, walking neither swiftly nor slowly. Five minutes later he was astride his horse and heading back to the distant Triangle herd.

But the instant he was out of sight of the Indian camp, he fed steel to his cayuse, lifting the mount to a fast gallop, for there was no guessing just how far the Comanche chieftain would go to protect him. Perhaps Rondeen's outfit was already into saddles, taking his trail. But there was no rolling drum of hoofbeats on the back trail, and he came in safety at long last to the sprawling sea of longhorns where Billy Wing awaited him.

His report to the oldster was brief but thorough, telling all that had happened, and Billy listened in appropriate silence and made very little comment afterward. But when they bedded down that night, Billy saw to it that word of Chan's adventure was circulated, and each man's tightened alertness was noticeable. When the dawn came and the riders had roped out their saddlers for the day, and the bedrolls had been tossed into the chuck wagon, Chan broached an idea born of the enemy's nearness.

"There's another route to the west, boys," he said. "When the Lazy-L took a herd up to Dodge City two years ago, we went astray and saw a little stretch of that half-acre of hell. Some of you here remember it. It'll mean a dry drive, but it might be one way of throwing Rondeen off the trail. We're going to try it."

Mitch alone frowned his disapproval. He'd kept to himself at the supper hour, passing no word with Chan, and since they'd taken different watches during the night, there'd been no opportunity for Mitch to reveal whatever mood he'd nourished since the episode of the day before. But now he framed quick words of protest.

"Head west!" he exclaimed. "Man, there's no water that direction until we hit the Canadian, a hundred miles from here, probably. It's no route for cattle!"

Chan gave him a surprised stare. "I don't recollect your being along on any Lazy-L drive, Mitch," he said. "How do you come to know so much about the kind of country that lies to the west of us?"

Mitch's frown deepened. "I've taken a little *pasear* a time or two," he said. "Do you think I've never got farther than shoutin' distance from the home spread?"

Here, then, was the explanation of where Mitch had been on some of those occasions Billy Wing had reported — the times when Mitch had vanished from the Lazy-L for lengthy periods. The question that crossed Chan's mind was whether Caesar Rondeen had been with him on those trips. But he didn't put his curiosity into words. The problems of the trail came first.

114

"We've got women along, Mitch," he said quietly. "This is one time when we've got to think of more than the herd. If the boys are against a dry drive, we'll call it off. Otherwise we're striking west."

He eyed the circle of faces as he spoke, but there was no dissenting shake of a head. These men would abide by the judgment of their trail boss, and so the matter was decided, the arrowhead aiming to the west once it was whipped into shape, the land turning drier and hotter as they plodded along. Gone was the succulent grass of a fairer land before that day was through, only the short-bladed buffalo grass growing here. And overhead the sun wheeled slowly in a lifeless sky, a brassy disc, malevolent and merciless.

New problems presented themselves in such a section. This arid land nourished nothing that could be used as fuel, and the supply of firewood which Stew Bidwell carried slung beneath the chuck wagon was gone by the second night. Even buffalo chips had become a priceless commodity, for the migratory herds of the shaggy beasts that the Texans called "humpbacked beef" had avoided this waterless way. So now Ollie Archer, the kid wrangler, had a new chore, heading into the low, fringing hills from time to time and snaking whatever wood he could find, back to the Lazy-L camp.

Now the nights gave no respite from the grueling grind of the day, for, with no water to be found in this lost land, the herd was driven three extra hours by starlight in the hopes of finding some forgotten stream. Even when camp was made, the cattle were far too restless to bed down, walking aimlessly in an everlasting circle for another hour or so until at last utter weariness forced them to their knees. Even then there were restless longhorns who refused to let the others rest, these recalcitrant ones milling by spells until Chan found it necessary to send the night-hawkers into the herd to break up the groups.

Before the dawn the outfit was on the move, stirred into sluggish action by the slight chance that moisture might have gathered on the skimpy grass during the night. Then the sun was aloft again, making a seat of torture out of a saddle, for leather soon grew too hot to touch. The hours blended one with another, having a hellish sameness to them, and a low moan began to rise from the restless longhorns, growing until it became an incessant plea, plaintive and compelling.

They came to the grave that day, a low mound of heaped rocks, a tiny upthrust against the prairie's flatness, and there was something grimly prophetic about the look of it. A crude marker reared above it, and Chan and Billy, angling for a better view, found a name scratched on the makeshift headboard, H. Thompson. No more than that, no date of birth or date of death, no saying how this lone wayfarer who'd been H. Thompson, once upon a distant time, had come here and gone no farther.

"Thompson," Billy Wing spelled out laboriously. "Why, Thunder on the Pecos, that must be old Hank Thompson a-restin' there. Do you remember about him, Chan, or was that while you was up in Montana? Thompson hailed from farther south than Rawson. He took a herd to Ogallala for him and a bunch o' his neighbors. Sold the beef in the north, paid off the trail crew he'd hired, and started back south with a satchel full o' money. Never was heard of again. There was some said he'd gone right on to Mexico with his own money, and his neighbors' as well. Wonder what done for him, and who buried him here?"

But the grave refused to answer, staying mute and silent, and the mystery of what had befallen Hank Thompson remained half a mystery. This was the way of the wasteland, Chan reflected, keeping its secrets to itself, gobbling up whatever dared trespass, and leaving only such somber warnings as this grave, for others who challenged it. And the grave had the same sobering influence on all who rode past it today, each rider giving it at least a glance, though Mitch rode by with his head averted. Holy Joe Hawkins stumbled from his horse to stand there half of a minute, his head bowed, his lips moving soundlessly.

Then the grave was behind them, whirling dust-devils obscuring the view of it, just as the memory of the dead was erased by the needs of the living.

The dry drive was leaving its mark on the humans as well as the cattle, Chan noticed. The men were growing morose and irritable, Jenny Rondeen was looking as haggard as of yore, and only Consuelo's beauty still blossomed beneath such a sun.

Stirred by a nameless concern, Chan fell abreast of Jenny's wagon that second day, forcing a note of levity into his voice as he asked, "A mighty nice trip, eh, mother? And to think that when we crossed the Red, I hoped I'd never see that much water again as long as I lived."

She shrugged, her parched lips forming into a humorless smile. "Here's a good place to take the cure," she observed. "Whiskey tastes like lava in this desert."

As on the occasion when they'd forded the Red at flood time, Chan was beginning to doubt the wisdom of his decision, for he'd brought those who'd followed him into this dread land in order to avoid another danger, and he wasn't so sure that the sacrifice had gained them anything. Twice Ollie Archer had reported mysterious figures near the remuda in a single night, and once Pete Still had fired at some phantom made of starlight and shadow on the night guard. Neither hand, though, had been able to swear that he'd seen anything but figments of his own feverish imagination.

Half the crew was soon riding point position. No longer was there a need to haze recalcitrant drags back to the herd. The longhorns had ceased grazing, moving forward stolidly as though realizing that their salvation lay somewhere up ahead, their walk growing faster until it became a run, and the job was to hold them back.

"Once let 'em get to lopin'," Billy Wing summarized, "and them critters'll run till they hit the Canadian or drop dead."

So now men who'd tasted the dust of the drag rode in the glory of point position, weaving to and fro before the leaders, holding them in check and gazing backward over that expanse of brown, bony backs. But with the herd held in check, the feverish, ungovernable leaders began turning back, wandering aimlessly, the drags overtaking the lead, and the longhorns lost all semblance of a trail herd. By dint of popping rope ends and sweaty toil, the riders managed to get them into shape again.

Often Chan loped on ahead, scouting to the right and left of the trail, hoping to find some sign of water in this arid wasteland. Yet always the panorama was the same before him, a limitless expanse of blistered nothingness made wavering and hazy by the heat. How many men, he wondered, had pitted themselves against this desert and lost? And musing thus, he tried to visualize a phantom parade of his predecessor — marauding savages, exploring Spaniards drawn by futile dreams of golden cities, buckskin-clad mountain men, westward-facing wagoners, trade-hungry merchants blazing a trail to the ancient City of the Holy Faith of Saint Francis, and naming that trail the Santa Fe . . .

He began to wonder if the heat haze that danced in the distance was wavering through his brain as well, and fell to brooding upon the irony of his own situation. What was he doing here, he demanded of himself? What business did he have hazing a herd through this forgotten inferno when he'd no longer be part of the Lazy-L once the herd reached Whispering and Mitch became master? And the injustice of it all grew to gigantic proportions in his fevered mind, until he snatched himself away from such thoughts with an effort, thrillingly aware of a miracle.

A breeze had touched his cheek! And lifting his eyes and gazing behind him, he saw every longhorn suddenly bolting into a broken, ungainly run, each of them veering directly north. No use now for the point riders to try and stay them, for only the hand of God could check that torrent of beef, as Billy Wing's quavering cry testified.

"The Canadian! The Canadian! It's just ahead, you rannyhans. Git outa the way, Chan! The Lazy-L's a-lopin' to water."

The Canadian River. Then Mitch had been mistaken when he'd guessed that the Canadian was a hundred miles away. Or Chan had lost all count of the days or the miles they'd covered in this wasteland. Now the longhorns were stampeding, and no mistake about it, but not a man made a move to stop them, knowing the stampede would come to an end at the river's edge. Chan's cue was to get out of the pathway, and he lifted his horse to a run, veering eastward. And that was when a rider came charging toward him, thundering out of the thicket of wild plum that fringed the Canadian.

Too long had Chan pitted himself against this merciless land to be properly alert. The dry days had stolen a measure of his faculties, and the oncoming rider was almost abreast of him before it percolated into his consciousness that it was Jube Cazborg. Only then did Chan realize that Pete Still and Ollie Archer had been right in their suspicion that Caesar Rondeen had stalked the Lazy-L along the waterless way.

For Jube Cazborg was here, his gun blazing as he came forward. Chan stiffened himself against the impact of lead, but it was his horse that was hit and was going down. Instinctively he kicked free of the stirrups, just as Cazborg wheeled his own mount and angled away, his swarthy face triumphant. For Chan had thrown himself clear of the horse, but now he lay sprawling in the very path of that oncoming juggernaut of thirst-crazed longhorns.

Chapter Eleven

With death thundering down upon him, Chan's impulse was to hug close to his dying horse in the flimsy hope that the herd might split and go around that threshing obstruction. The ways of cattle are unpredictable, for there is very little logic in a longhorn. But just now every ounce of that onrushing beef was possessed of a single, dominating idea — to get to the river beyond as quickly as possible. A mountain wouldn't stop them in their madness, so Chan staggered to his feet and began to run, cold with the certainty that there could be only one outcome to such a race.

Ahead of him, Jube Cazborg was already disappearing into the thicket from which he'd emerged, and Chan had a glimpse of three or four waiting riders putting spurs to their horses and angling away, the black-garbed figure of Caesar Rondeen one of them.

Beneath Chan the earth seemed to tremble, and when he cast a frantic glance behind, he saw the longhorns as a solid body moving down upon him. His running became mechanical then, pointless and nightmarish, for he knew he was doomed and that his efforts were only averting the inevitable for a few moments. And then a rider was alongside him, shouting something that was lost beneath the rumble of hoofs, his hand reaching to hook under Chan's left armpit.

Getting up behind the saddle was something that Chan was never able to remember coherently afterwards, and his rescuer had spurred forward, crossing the open stretch and driving his mount over the bank of the Canadian and into the river before Chan realized it was Mitch who'd come to his aid.

At first that made no sense, until he recalled that Mitch, like many others, had been riding point position, trying to hold back the thirsty longhorns. Mitch, then, had seen his peril and been in a position to lend a hand.

None of which changed the fact that Mitch Loring had saved his foster-brother's life at the risk of his own, for the cue of every rider had been to get out of the way when that beef started bolting forward. Gratitude became a swelling lump, choking Chan, but there was no time now to put it into words.

Caesar Rondeen and the few satellites who'd accompanied him had long since vanished from sight, and no move was made on the part of the Lazy-L to give chase. Probably Rondeen had been hovering as close to the drive as he dared, waiting a chance to bedevil the Lazy-L. Here on the bank of the Canadian, fate had placed an opportunity in Rondeen's hands, and Cazborg, hungry for revenge, had struck a blow — with or without his master's sanction. But the plan had failed. Caesar Rondeen might strike again, but in the meantime the Triangle drovers were far too interested in the miracle of water after the dusty stretch of the wasteland to care whether Rondeen escaped scot-free or not.

The cattle had plunged through the thicket, spilled over the bank, and were out into the stream now, standing belly-deep in the water, yet none lowered their heads to drink. Whereupon Billy Wing, seeing that wisdom born of bovine instinct, called the attention of the crew to this queer action.

"Learn a lesson from yon critters, boys," he bellowed. "Thunder on the Pecos, them longhorns ain't gonna git stomach cramps by swillin' water after a dry drive. Now don't none of you go provin' that you got less brains than a longhorn."

His advice was heeded, men contenting themselves with stripping off gunbelts and boots and plunging into the river, there to drink sparingly at first, but whooping and hollering like so many Comanches let loose, and splashing about in the water as though it were an element they'd never seen before. And after the longhorns had eventually drunk to their heart's content and crossed to the shady thickets on the north bank, the men stretched themselves luxuriously on the shore and opined that hell was a good place for a man to get out of.

It was then that Chan had his chance to speak to Mitch, but when he began to put his stumbling thanks into words, Mitch cut him short with a brusque gesture.

"Chan, when your horse went down, no man happened to be closer to you than me," Mitch said. "If I'd let you get trampled to death when I might have saved you, it would be just the same as if I'd murdered you. It happens I'm not a killer. But keep your thanks to yourself. And don't go gettin' the idea that what happened today changes anything between us. What I said back in the Territory still goes."

Turning, Mitch strode away, Chan looking after him and remembering many things out of the days when they'd been boys together. But though part of his heart called after that handsome, arrogant youngster who'd once been his brother, his lips remained locked. And when Stew Bidwell prepared a special repast that evening to celebrate the end of the dry drive, both Lorings ate in morose silence, each studiously avoiding the eyes of the other.

But, as before, their animosities must wait, for the drive was far from finished. And the herd headed on with another dawn, threading through a country flat as the wastelands, but well watered by streams flowing out of the west, some joining the Canadian behind them, some emptying into the Cimarron which lay ahead. Then there came the day when the Cimarron was crossed and they were into Kansas, and soon they were seeing what was to any drover the devil's own invention — the barbed-wire barriers of the grangers.

That Kansas border was a quarantine line, and it was here that trail herds were often stopped and inspected for the dread Spanish, or Texas, fever which wrought havoc among homesteaders' beef. Though the longhorns were immune to the disease, they carried with them a tick that dropped off and infected granger cattle which used the same bedding ground.

But no officers put in an appearance this far west on the border, and Chan breathed easier. His clearance papers were in order, proof enough that his herd was disease-free, but granger lawmen were often a skeptical lot, and to have the herd quarantined for inspection might mean losing anywhere from a week to a month or better.

Fort Faraday would wait until the allotted date for soldier beef, but probably not a day longer. There were many herds going north this season, and if the Lazy-L should fail to complete its bargain on time, the contract would be re-let to the first drover who was interested. That point had been made plain enough when Chan had talked to the commanding officer. Therefore Chan crossed Kansas soil as a man treads upon egg-shells, anxious to be through and beyond lest trouble rear itself to delay them.

Thus the longhorns were swung ever westward, avoiding the fences that wrapped themselves around a hundred homesteads, just as the Texas Trail itself had veered toward the setting sun, pushed west by the encroaching grangers, so that Wichita, Abilene, and Ellsworth had each in their turn been famous trail's-end towns, relinquishing that dubious honor at long last to hell-roaring Dodge City, toughest of them all.

"Thunder on the Pecos," Billy Wing said one day as they threaded among the checkerboard of farms that mottled the prairie, "this would be a fine time for Caesar Rondeen to brew hisself up some deviltry. He knows this north trail, every inch of it. He's proved that time and again. And he knows what it would do to our chances if we got stopped. If he should put a bee in the ear of some badge-totin' hoeman. . . ."

To which Chan nodded solemnly, for Billy Wing had voiced his own latest fear, the thing that kept him tense and alert these June days.

He'd even taken to keeping an eye on Consuelo whenever they stopped for the night, remembering that she, too, had reason to want to see these longhorns fail to reach Montana, and knowing that she might easily slip away and report them to Kansas law. He hated himself for spying, and for the suspicion that prompted him to do so, but he had no other choice.

He'd had very little to say to the girl lately. She kept to Jenny Rondeen's wagon in the evenings, as though sensing that her presence at the campfire might put a restraint upon the rough-talking cowhands in that only hour they could call their own. Often enough Mitch kept her company at such times, perching upon the wagon tongue while their voices chimed together and low laughter floated back to Chan upon the night breeze. And because Chan had loved this girl from the moment he'd first seen her up in Montana, he fell to reflecting upon the irony of a destiny that had devised another difference between him and his foster-brother.

They took to driving by starlight again, even

as they'd done on the dry drive, for the law was more apt to be abroad by day, and those stolen hours were therefore the safest to travel. But there came a night when they found a county line fence which apparently stretched straight for endless miles to block them. Here they held a brief consultation, deciding upon ways and means of passing this barrier. For hours their trail had been no better than a narrow, crooked lane with very little graze for the cattle, and it was senseless to turn back.

"We could cut the damn' fence," Mitch suggested. "Me, I'm getting tired of zig-zagging all over creation."

But Chan over-ruled such a drastic measure. "There's bound to be a gate somewhere," he said. "We'll get the boys to milling the herd. They can hold it here while we go and have a look-see."

So shortly afterwards the two Lorings, along with Billy Wing, rode to the east, flanking the fence. Riding together, they found a gate no more than a mile from where the herd was held waiting. But two men stood guard before it, and though they wore overalls and cotton shirts, there was no denying the authority of the badges pinned upon them, or the threat of the shotgun one held in his hands to back up any argument the pair might have to make.

With the Lazy-L riders facing these mild-mannered men, it was like two conflicting forces being personified — the Man on Horseback, and the Man with the Hoe — the first the representative of cattleland's many-acred might, the second the embodiment of a force that would yet humble the horseman in the dust, building a new empire passively, and enduring by sheer force of swarming numbers.

"Heading some place, Texans?" the one with the shotgun asked, eyeing their gear speculatively. "Who are you, and what's your outfit?"

"Lazy-L," Chan answered instinctively, for too long had that been his brand for his tongue to take to the Triangle with ease. "From south of the Brazos." And because the inevitable had happened and there could be no avoiding it, he added truthfully, "Our herd's being held a mile or so to the west. We've been looking for a gate."

"You've found it," the granger said. "But we'll have to look over your stock for signs of fever ticks. That is, unless you've got clearance papers to show they were examined before leaving Texas. We're not here to make trouble, cowboy. We're just protecting this stretch of farmland."

Whereupon Chan breathed a gusty sigh of relief, for once again the anticipation of trouble had been greater than the actuality. There'd be no delaying quarantine! He reached for the water-tight wallet that had held his clearance papers all the way from Texas, but reaching, he stiffened in his saddle. For the wallet was no longer in his chap's pocket!

In that first black moment, the wallet's disappearance was a mystery, baffling and unexplainable, until memory came back to him with a rush, bringing a solution. That Comanche camp! They'd searched him for weapons there, after the struggle when he'd been made a captive. He supposed that they'd taken only his guns, and those had been restored to him afterwards by Caesar Rondeen. But the wallet had been lifted, too, possibly by some nimble-fingered Comanche buck who'd suspected that it contained money and who understood the power of that green paper among white men.

"I'm sorry," Chan said and knew that to try and explain would be futile. "I've lost my clearance papers somewhere along the trail."

"Is that so?" the man with the shotgun scoffed, and suspicion drew the slackness out of his features, leaving them taut and determined. "I said we weren't looking for trouble, cowboy, but we don't like people trying to fool us. We'll just have to put that herd of yours under quarantine until we look it over. Lead the way to it."

Thus had the shadow of trouble been dispelled, only to lay its black swathe upon the Lazy-L once again. And the starlight's sullen glint on the shotgun's barrels made a mute reminder that these granger officers held the power to enforce their edict.

Chapter Twelve

When Mitch had suggested cutting the fence, Chan had vetoed the idea, knowing there might be trouble enough without deliberately inviting it by such roughshod procedure. But now, facing these granger officers and hearing their decree, Chan realized that the worst had befallen the Lazy-L, and any gamble would be better than meekly submitting to the delay of quarantine. That was why he shaped a desperate plan and put it into operation — a grim gamble, with death sitting in the dealer's chair.

"Wait a moment," he cried and stepped down from his saddle, pawing into his chaps pocket again and producing an old envelope, made soggy and undecipherable by many river crossings. "Here's those clearance papers. I had them after all."

"First you had 'em, then you didn't — and now you've got 'em again," the man with the shotgun said disgustedly. "Are you drunk, cowboy, or loco?"

But he lowered his shotgun barrel and leaned forward for a better look — which was exactly what Chan was hoping he'd do. Thus the granger was off-guard, and his jaw was an easy target when Chan let go with a looping right.

The shotgun blared at the ground as the man went down, and mingled with the roar of it was Chan's strident, "Jump the other one, boys!"

Hurling himself upon the man with the gun, he wrenched the weapon away even as he flattened the granger to the earth. At the same time Mitch and Billy Wing came out of their saddles, Mitch catapulting himself from his kak full upon the other peace officer. For a moment there was a confused tangle of arms and legs, until the Lazy-L men came to their feet, panting but triumphant.

"Out, both of them," Chan observed, his elation tempered by regret because necessity had given him no choice but to do this thing.

"What are you figgerin' on doing?" Billy Wing wheezed.

"Tie these fellows and gag them," Chan said. "Then we'll run the herd through this gate."

"And have every lawman in Kansas swarming onto our trail!" Mitch ejaculated. "We'd never get away with such a deal!"

Chan shrugged. "It's worth a try," he decided. "I told them we were Lazy-L, remember. That was a slip of the tongue, but it means the law will be looking for the Lazy-L, not the Triangle. And now that we're nearing Dodge, there'll be dozens of herds on the main trail. With luck, we may be out of granger country before anybody else asks for a look at our clearance papers. They were taken away from me back at that Comanche camp, I reckon."

Whereupon the light of enthusiasm came into Mitch's eyes, his silence an admission that he saw the wisdom of Chan's way. It was another gamble, of course, grim as the one Chan had made when he'd jumped a loaded shotgun. But there was everything to be gained by it.

"Billy, you go back and fetch the herd," Chan ordered. "Me and Mitch will tie up these gents and drag them off to one side of the gate. They haven't seen the herd, or any of the crew, and it's a damn small glimpse they had of us by starlight. Tomorrow they'll know a herd went through this way, but that's about all they'll know. And since the gate's apparently guarded day and night, the guards who come next morning will find these gents and untie them."

Chuckling softly, Billy vaulted into his saddle, thundering into the west. When he returned with the herd behind him, the streaming longhorns shaped into a narrow wedge by the drivers, the gate was open, and

Chan and Mitch were waiting beside it, both minus belts and neckerchiefs, for those articles had been used to bind and gag the granger officers. Soon the longhorns were flowing through the gate, the wagons rumbling after them. Then the Lazy-L was forging onward, a fugitive drive now, four thousand longhorns beyond the law.

There was no bedding down that night, the cattle being pushed through all of the dark hours, veering steadily eastward, and the second dawn after Chan's clash with Kansas law found them on the main trail for the first time since they'd left Texas. Dust plumes rose to the north and south of them, for here a dozen trail herds, starting from as many separate points, had finally converged.

"The law's been travelin' a heap faster than us," Billy Wing observed. "Hossbackers has carried the word ahead to be on the watch for us. But there's shore enough herds hereabouts to keep any badgetoter busy cuttin' sign for a Lazy-L."

"Chances are they won't bother checking on the trail," Chan guessed. "They'll figger any herd headin' this way is bound to stop at Dodge. That's where we'll have to keep our eye peeled for the law."

Already he was contemplating skirting Dodge City, for his destination was far to the north, and there was no real need to tarry at that famous town. But since the crossing of the Canadian, there'd been talk of nothing else among the crew but Dodge City, men who'd been there speaking of the myriad pleasures and excitements of that fabulous place, others eagerly anticipating their first visit.

To deprive the crew of such a holiday would be a rank injustice, poor compensation for their loyalty along the thundering trail. Besides, avoiding the town when they were this close to it would be an act so extraordinary that it might easily draw suspicion's fingers toward them.

Thus, on the day that smoke laid a black smudge along the northern horizon, a token that yonder ran the railroad to Dodge, Chan made his decision, and that decision was to give his crew a taste of the pleasures they hadn't known for nearly sixty days. As dusk settled, they splashed across the wide, muddy Arkansas River and bedded the longhorn herd just beyond the north bank. And here Chan had a talk with Consuelo, broaching a matter that had given him cause for concern.

"You'll want to go into Dodge, I reckon," Chan said. "Whether we stay overnight or not, it will be nice for you and the *Señora* Rondeen to enjoy a hotel room and a bath. Likewise, you might want to do some shopping at the stores. But I've been wondering —"

"Yes, *señor?*" Was she laughing at him?

"You know what happened the night we went through that county line fence," Chan blurted. "You couldn't help but know. We let the crew know what happened to a pair of granger officers that was guarding the gate, and there was plenty of campfire talk about it. What I'm wanting, Consuelo, is your word that you won't head straight for the closest lawman if I let you go into Dodge City."

The laughter went out of her eyes. "You do not need the promise, *señor,*" she said stiffly. "Pah, thees is our fight, yours and mine, this fight for Whispering Basin. I don't get no damn lawman to help me, *sabe?* Now you can quit watching my wagon at night, like the scarecrow guarding the corn!"

He had to chuckle, but the levity went out of him with another thought, and he said very seriously, "Thank you, *señorita.* And you can do a great favor for me, if you will. The *Señora* Rondeen will be with you in Dodge. They call her Whiskey Jenny, Consuelo, and not without cause. If you could sorta see —"

"I understand," she said, and her solemnity matched his. "I will keep her from the drinking, *señor.* Be sure of that."

There was nothing more to be said, and very shortly Consuelo and Jenny Rondeen took their wagon on into Dodge, and Billy Wing, who'd gone on ahead, sent on a special mission by Chan, came back to report.

"She's the same old Dodge," Billy said. "Wild and woolly and full of fleas. But I kept an ear to the ground, like you said, and there didn't seem to be no great excitement about any owl-hoot outfit that tied up a pair of peace officers down south. But Caesar Rondeen's in Dodge. He's been there for several days, restin' up, likely. His wagons is pulled in behind the Drover's Saloon, and I hear tell he's took rooms over that outfit."

"You've all heard what Billy's said," Chan told the assembled crew. "Watch yourselves in town, boys; and remember that you've never heard of the Lazy-L. You're the Triangle outfit. Three or four of you have got to stay here with the herd. Who's volunteering?"

Billy Wing had already had his taste of Dodge, and Stew Bidwell opined that he could do without city life and make a hand meanwhile. Holy Joe Hawkins, muttering something about Sodom and Gomorrah, likewise elected to stay away from yon citadel of sin. But, surprisingly, Mitch also volunteered to remain behind. Knowing Mitch's love for the glitter of lights upon glassware and the camaraderie of the card tables, Chan was openly astonished, but made no remark.

There was the business of doling out money to the crew who drew upon their wages, Chan clambering into the chuck wagon for the strong box that had been King Loring's, and fishing its key from his shirt pocket. In this box was money and the homestead entry papers that gave the Lazy-L a claim on Whispering, and Chan's regret was that he hadn't put the herd's clearance papers into this massive box instead of carrying them in his wallet.

Once money was passed out, the outfit was into saddles, Chan in the lead, and bee-lining into Dodge City, whooping and hollering as they came — men starved for pleasure who saw the feast spread before them in the false fronts of this turbulent town.

And here it was — this town that had once been called Buffalo City, and which had seen in their turns the buffalo-hunters, the railroad labor crews, the soldiers from Fort Dodge five miles eastward, and, finally that breed that swarmed up out of the southland, the Texas trail drovers, the lustiest of them all — those men who'd come across the thundering miles to buck the tiger and dance with painted women, swaggering from saloon to saloon, easy prey for the vultures who grew fat upon the sons of toil and sweat. And above the town, dominating an adjoining rise, was Boot Hill cemetery, mute and ominous reminder that some came here never to depart.

In the manner of Texas men, the Lazy-L crowded their horses to a full gallop right through the packed plaza where a flood of brilliance poured from open doors and windows and from the glassed-in coal-oil lamps perched atop poles at every corner. Then they racked their horses before a Front Street saloon, and Chan turned his pack loose with a flourish of his hand.

"Leave a drop or two for me," he grinned. "I'm seeing a barber who's going to have to have a strong arm and a sharp razor. Tap 'er light, boys."

In the barber shop he awaited his turn, for all of the long row of chairs were occupied. Afterwards, sheared and shaved, he enjoyed the luxury of a bath, then came to the street, walking along beneath the wooden awnings and skirting the barrels of water that had been placed at convenient intervals in case of fire, feeling the press of life all about him and savoring it as a strange thing long removed from his existence, hearing the continual rumble of sound that gave this town the name of being hell-roaring.

He was at loss as to what to do. Responsibility kept him from cutting loose in the manner of his men, though he did elbow to

142

one bar, toying with a drink and finding it not to his taste. He tarried before the three stories of the Dodge Opera House, but there was no show tonight, and at last he decided to go back to the herd and relieve Mitch if his foster-brother now had a mind to see a bit of city life.

But yonder came Mitch, stalking surreptitiously along the street.

At first Chan couldn't credit his eyes, but there was no mistaking that handsome face. Chan's first thought, then, was that something had gone wrong over there on the bank of the Arkansas and Mitch had come to tell him about it. Possibly the law had appeared and was demanding a look at those missing clearance papers. But something about the furtive manner of Mitch told Chan differently. Mitch Loring wasn't trying to locate anyone. Rather, he was doing his best to keep from being noticed. As Chan watched, Mitch stopped a wayfarer and put a question to him. The man spoke at length, pointing often toward the south as he did, and Mitch nodded and headed in that direction.

Drawn by curiosity, Chan followed after him, heading into Hell's Half Acre, that region of hurdy-gurdy houses, brothels, and gambling dens of the worst sort that lay south of the Santa Fe tracks. Here he saw Mitch pause before a noisy edifice bearing the legend DROVER'S SALOON. This, then, had been the place Mitch had been seeking when he'd asked the wayfarer for directions. But Mitch didn't go inside the saloon, turning instead and skirting the building to the rear, Chan close at his heels but managing to keep unnoticed, which was easy enough since it was darker than the inside of a steer's stomach here in the alleyway behind.

Yonder, in the saloon's back yard, were four wagons, and even if Chan hadn't seen them before, back in the camp of the Comanches in the Nations, he'd have known whose property they were, since Billy Wing had reported that Caesar Rondeen had taken quarters over the Drover's Saloon. And now Mitch was vanishing into one of those wagons, staying there overly long but finally coming into view only to disappear into another wagon.

Patently he was searching for something, and it came to Chan that Mitch's volunteering to stay with the herd had been a subterfuge to enable Mitch to come into Dodge alone. Had he loped in with the crew, one or two of them might have stayed in his company, and Mitch hadn't wanted that.

Now he was here, but his actions made no sense to Chan. What desperate need was driving Mitch in his search? Chan didn't know;

but now Mitch, his efforts apparently futile so far, was standing silently, scanning the darkened rear of the building before him.

The saloon was a two-story affair, and a shed clung to the rear of it, just below the upper windows. Moving forward cautiously, Mitch began to climb, crawling to the roof of the shed where he paused at the window, waist-high to him, and tested it. Then the window was up, and Mitch was vanishing through it. And with his foster-brother gone from sight, Chan was instantly after him, climbing as silently as he could until he finally stood on the shed's roof.

The window was still open, and Mitch was in the room beyond, so intent upon whatever had fetched him here that he hadn't heard any sound Chan might have made. Now Mitch sighed, a gusty sigh of satisfaction, scratching a match aglow and bending to examine something he held in his hand. In that fitful flare Chan had a brief glimpse of the room, seeing a bed and a scattering of furniture, and seeing the thing Mitch had come after — the black metal box that belonged to Caesar Rondeen.

And this was the moment when a door opened on the far side of the room, a man bulking big, silhouetted by the dim light of the hallway behind him, two other men crowding into view at his back.

"Raise your hands!" the voice of Caesar Rondeen ordered raspingly. "I thought I heard someone stirring in here, just before I opened the door. Jube, get his guns away from him. Doc, light a lamp. *Steady, stranger.* I've got a gun lined right at your brisket."

Then they were all into the room, Chan bobbing his head below the window sill as Doc Menafee touched a match to a lamp wick and light blossomed. But as Caesar Rondeen gasped in surprise, Chan doffed his sombrero and risked another look.

"Why, it's our old *amigo,* Mitch Loring," Caesar Rondeen said. "And up to a bit of petty thievery, too. Hand over that box, Mitch. So that's what fetched you here. I never dreamed you'd have the nerve."

"I've got the nerve all right," Mitch countered defiantly. "And I've grown tired of living on the lip of a volcano that may explode any minute. Here's your box, Rondeen, and to hell with you. Play your damn ace any time you please, for all I care."

They presented a grim tableau, Mitch standing there with fists clenched, Rondeen absently fingering the box which Mitch had passed over to him, Jube Cazborg and Doc Menafee, both without bandages, Chan noticed, standing slaunch-wise, the one, big-bodied and swarthy, the other tall and stringy,

146

both of them like wolves waiting the signal to close in for the kill.

"You're a distressing problem, Mitchell," Caesar Rondeen said thoughtfully. "You've become a desperate man, by your own admission, and I dislike the thought of having to guard against you from here on out. Also, you seem to have matured a bit on the trail. Once I thought you'd be one Loring I wouldn't have to bother killing, since you were sliding down to hell as fast as you could under your own power. But I'm afraid you're becoming dangerous."

"When you killed the King, I told you how I stood," Mitch said. "There'll be powder smoke between us some day, Rondeen. Don't forget that."

Caesar Rondeen passed a hand through his sweep of salt-and-pepper hair, and with the gesture he came to a decision. "Jube, take him out, you and Doc," he ordered. "He's one Loring that isn't worth my personal attention. Get him out of my sight, boys. He's making me weary. About a mile from town should do. You understand."

They understood him. No doubt about that. The proof of it was in Jube Cazborg's wolfish grin. And Chan understood, too, knowing that death stood at Mitch's shoulder, and that in another moment he'd be taken through the doorway and away to his doom.

There were three targets for a man's gun in that room, but Chan chose a fourth, laying his gun along the window sill and blasting away at the lamp. When it crashed out, he was tossing a leg over the sill, plunging into the room in the descending darkness.

Chapter Thirteen

The thing that saved Chan Loring's life in that first moment inside the room was the element of surprise, for pandemonium reigned in the sudden darkness, and there was no way Rondeen or his men could tell friend from foe. But with faint moonlight touching the bulk of Jube Cazborg, Chan laid his gun-barrel alongside the man's head, dumping him to the floor. At the same time Doc Menafee's voice shrilled loudly.

"It's Chan Loring," the lean gunhawk cried. "Caesar, don't let 'em get through the door."

Rondeen, a lean shadow-shape, moved quickly to prevent an exit, and Chan, lunging across the room, almost fell over a chair. Grasping the piece of furniture, he hurled it toward the dim outline of the window through which he'd entered, and part of the sash was carried away as glass showered.

"One of them's gone through the window," Rondeen's voice barked, and the lean shadow-shape moved again, this time away from the door. Thus Chan cleared the pathway to escape.

He still clutched his gun, but he didn't fire again because Mitch was some place in the room, no telling where. Jube Cazborg loomed large and grotesque, for he was on his hands and knees, cursing loudly, but Rondeen and Doc Menafee had sagely fallen silent, thereby making their whereabouts uncertain.

Rondeen was probably still clutching that metal box, and Chan wished mightily to get his hands on it, a wish that was obviously shared by Mitch. But this wasn't the time to make such a try, so he darted for the door instead risking a whispered "Mitch," which betrayed the fact that both Lorings were still in the room.

But at least Chan's window-breaking ruse had gotten Caesar Rondeen away from the door. Wrenching it open, Chan bolted into the dimly-lighted hallway. Mitch was right at his heels, proof enough that he'd understood Chan's strategy. Together they sprinted for the stairway at the end of the hall, the steps leading downward to the barroom.

They'd escaped from the room, but danger still dogged them. Already Caesar Rondeen and his men were bobbing into the hallway, firing as they came, their guns thundering loudly in the confines of the building, the walls hurling back the echoes. Pausing, Chan laid a high shot behind him, the snarl of lead discouraging Rondeen in mid-stride.

Then the two Lorings were leaping down the stairway, taking the steps two at a time, bolting into the barroom, where startled glances met them. Those shots had told every saloon patron that trouble was on the loose, but no one had completely grasped the situation, and no move was made to block the fleeing pair.

"This way," Mitch panted, and jerked at Chan's elbow, veering him toward a rear doorway. Through it, they found themselves behind the Drover's Saloon, in the big back yard where Rondeen's wagons stood. But they didn't tarry here, sprinting down the alley instead, thundering along side by side until they drew to a stop, panting and gasping. If they had gone from the yard back to the street by the way which both of them had come earlier in the evening, success might have attended their efforts to escape. But here they faced a fence too high to be easily scaled, finding themselves blocked by this wooden barrier.

"They're coming after us," Mitch cried, and when Chan strained his ears, pounding feet testified that men were streaming out of the saloon, dozens of them, spreading out to trap the fugitives. Caesar Rondeen, it seemed, was not without friends in Dodge City.

And the strategy of Rondeen was all too

apparent. Thwarted in his attempt to do away with Mitch, Rondeen was now trying to salvage an even better opportunity out of tonight's defeat. Here were two Lorings almost within his grasp — the one who was King Loring's kin, and the one who'd pledged his loyalty to the King regardless of alien blood ties. Once *both* of these Lorings were out of the way, the Lazy-L would never lay claim to Whispering. That was the way Caesar Rondeen was undoubtedly reasoning, Chan guessed, and that was why Rondeen was striving to hem them in.

And Rondeen would likely succeed. No chance to about-face and head back down the alleyway. In that direction lay the Drover's Saloon — and the gravest danger. But Chan, his eyes roving desperately, striving to pierce the enveloping gloom, saw a new chance for them. Yonder stood a cluster of trash barrels, and Chan reached them quickly, tugging at a barrel and striving to roll it up against the fence.

"Mitch," he gasped. "Lend a hand."

Instantly Mitch was beside him, and together they worked, inching the ponderous barrel toward the fence. Then they were mounting the barrel, reaching from this precarious perch for a hold on the fence's top. Straining and panting, each managed to throw a leg over the pickets, hoist himself upward and drop down the other side.

But now they were in another alley, dark as the one they'd quitted. Boots were still beating along to the left and right of them, the sound dim in the distance, yet close enough to be a grim reminder that they were far from being in the clear. They moved forward stealthily, and all around them rose the roar of Dodge, strident reminder that in the midst of men they were alone and beyond help. In this shadowy realm south of the Santa Fe tracks, a man's troubles were nobody else's concern.

The end of the alleyway was just ahead, but here a lanky form loomed to block their way. Only one man had chosen to guard this point, but Chan was clammy with the thought that a single shout would bring others sprinting to the spot. Therefore, Chan gave the man no chance to shout.

Lashing out with his fist, Chan managed to find the fellow's jaw in the dark, and as the man went down, Chan was on top of him. But there was no need for that. The man beneath him was unconscious.

"Him!" Mitch exclaimed, as the moon edged out of a fleecy cloud bank and a vagrant beam touched the fallen man's face. "The kingpin."

"Rondeen, all right," Chan said, and, in spite of himself, he felt a small stab of regret because once again he'd laid hands on this renegade uncle of his.

"The box," Mitch whispered quickly. "Has he got the box with him?"

Chan's fingers groped in the shadows.

"Doesn't seem to be here," he announced. "He probably left it in the Drover's Saloon before he come hunting us. But it would be too risky going back for it, and he maybe hid it, anyway. Wait —"

Inspired by a new thought, he was going through Rondeen's pockets, and somewhere in the search his fingers touched a familiar object.

"For a one-eyed man, Rondeen sees just about everything," Chan observed as he held his own wallet aloft. "There was only a Chinaman's chance that he might have noticed one of the Comanches with my wallet and talked the buck out of it afterwards. And here it is."

"But are those clearance papers in it?" Mitch demanded. "Don't you reckon he destroyed them first thing?"

Chan had the wallet open, was probing its contents. "A great man for hanging onto anything that might be used as an ace, Rondeen," Chan remarked. "Maybe he thought he might

154

get us into some kind of a tight spot along the trail where he'd be able to make us a dicker if he had these papers to offer. They're here, Mitch."

"Then let's be moving," Mitch said, and shuddered. "No telling how many of his wolves are prowling around."

The two made their way to the street, no one challenging them en route, and, once into the stream of humanity that flowed along the boardwalks, each drew a breath of relief, for here was comparative safety, since the crowd made them inconspicuous. Thus they came out of Hell's Half Acre and to the plaza where Mitch had left his mount, and Chan took his from the hitch rail before the saloon where he'd parted company with the Lazy-L cowhands.

With no words between them, the pair pointed their Cayuses toward the bedding grounds on the bank of the Arkansas. The moon had broken completely free of its cloudy prison when they reached the herd, and Chan instantly spied the canvas tops of the wagons.

"Looks like Consuelo and Jenny have had their fill of Dodge," he observed. "They've come back."

"And some one else, too," Mitch added. "Who's the stranger talking to Stew Bidwell?"

Chan didn't know, but he wasn't left in

doubt for long. The man who stood by his own saddler, deep in conversation with the cook, was garbed in black, only his shirt front glimmering whitely. And upon it was a badge.

"Here he is now," Stew Bidwell spoke up as Chan slid out of his saddle. "This is our trail boss, mister. You can ask him what you want to know."

The stranger smiled. "I'm marshal of Dodge," he said and thereby proclaimed himself as belonging to that illustrious company that had included Ed Masterson and Wyatt Earp and Mysterious Dave Mather and many others who had, in their turn, kept the peace in the toughest town on earth.

"Glad to know you," Chan said, extending his hand and wondering the while if this man's presence here indicated some new move of Caesar Rondeen's.

"My business tonight isn't strictly in my line," the marshal admitted. "But I lend a hand to the county officers once in a while. Maybe you heard that some outfit calling itself the Lazy-L attacked two deputies down south when the boys demanded to see the outfit's clearance papers. According to the story the deputies told when they were untied by the relief guard next morning, the trail boss claimed he'd lost his clearance papers. Just a matter of routine, we're checking all herds that come this way."

"A good idea, sir," Chan said, and reached for his wallet. "Here's my papers. As you can see, we're the Triangle outfit. I think you'll find everything in order."

The marshal's inspection was brief. "Sorry to have troubled you," he said. "Good night."

Chan shot a glance at Stew Bidwell, and because that worthy wrangler of pots and pans had the sick look of a man who's just swallowed a quid of chewing tobacco, Chan had to grin. And with the marshal into his saddle and riding away, Chan was still grinning as he swung his eyes to Mitch.

Tonight the two of them had looked upon death together and come through unscathed, and Chan's hope was that the test of fire had dissolved the old differences. But Mitch's lips had resumed their sullen cast.

"I know what you're thinking, Chan," he said. "Now it's my turn to mumble some thanks. But I don't see it that way. I saved your carcass on the bank of the Canadian — and I've told you why I did it. You saved mine tonight. The way I see it, that squares things all around — and puts us right back where we started."

Whereupon Chan hid the deep hurt within him behind a careless shrug.

"Any way you want it, Mitch," he said, and

turned to stride away.

But Mitch detained him. "Wait," Mitch said slowly. "There's something I've got to tell you, Chan. After all, there's one job we both want to see finished, the job the King laid out. But the worst miles are still ahead. Don't ask me how I come to know so much about Caesar Rondeen's affairs, but believe me when I tell you that he's really ready to hit at us now."

"Meaning?" Chan invited.

"Meaning that he didn't dare do more than nip at our heels before," Mitch went on. "He didn't have enough guns behind him to buck the Lazy-L down south. But you saw how many men came stampeding out of the Drover's Saloon after us tonight to run us down."

"Bar-flys," Chan judged. "Galoots who wanted to get in on the excitement."

"I wish you were right," Mitch said with a shake of his head. "Listen, Chan. Rondeen's Spur Wheel Saloon down in Rawson was just a blind for his real business — which is heading a pack of twenty or more trail wolves up here in the north, gents who make a business of raiding herds. The outfit holes up here in Dodge, and Rondeen has caught up with them at last. You're the gent who gives the orders, Chan. Take my advice and round up our crew and get pointed out of here tonight. Caesar Rondeen's grown a real set of fangs since he hit Dodge City."

Chapter Fourteen

Over to the east, the lights of Dodge City made a sulphurous smear against the horizon, and here on the north bank of the Arkansas the Lazy-L herd milled restlessly, the cursing riders who'd had their holiday curtailed, forcing the cattle to their feet and preparing for a night drive. For Chan was taking Mitch's advice. He'd sent Billy Wing into town to collect the crew, routing the reluctant hands out of saloons and hurdy-gurdy houses, and now they were going to steal a march on Caesar Rondeen by shaking the dust of Dodge from their heels as soon as they could.

All of which was indication enough that Chan considered Mitch's warning as something worth heeding. Much remained shrouded in mystery, but at least it was obvious that Mitch Loring knew a great deal more about the north trail than anyone had ever suspected. He'd proved it down in the Nations by objecting to a dry drive, and tonight he'd confessed to intimate knowledge of Caesar Rondeen's shady affairs.

Also, Mitch was a man with a guilty conscience; and there was one thing Chan now knew for sure. The contents of that mysterious metal box of Caesar Rondeen's pertained to Mitch Loring. Rondeen had intimated as much in the camp of the Comanches, and Mitch's efforts to obtain the box tonight indicated that he desperately wanted possession of it.

There had been a day when Chan might have gone to Mitch and asked him outright to explain himself — a brother offering to share a brother's troubles. But that day was long since past. Each mile of the trail had widened the gap between them, though at least they shared a determination to do the King's will. And tonight they worked together to move the herd beyond the reach of Rondeen's trail wolves.

Thus Dodge City fell behind them, and when they finally bedded the herd in the darkness before dawn, the nighthawks rode with wary eyes and ready guns.

They made long drives in the days that followed, the level floor of northen Kansas flowing behind them, and often as not Chan left the pointing of the herd to Billy Wing and rode miles to the rear, anxiously scanning the flat grassland to the south for the first sign of marauders.

But, as though in contrition for the waywardness of past days, the trail smiled upon them now, keeping the peace as they forded the Republican River into Nebraska. Since most of the Texas drovers had brought their herds only as far as Dodge, the Triangle was alone now, even as it had been south of Kansas, a blunt arrowhead of longhorns stretched across a limitless vista of grass-carpeted emptiness, a cavalcade of cattle and men moving through a world all their own.

But where was Caesar Rondeen? That was the question tormenting Chan, the very absence of his renegade uncle giving him more cause for concern than if Rondeen had appeared with his pack. And Rondeen was bound to strike again. Thwarted in Dodge City, he'd be more eager than ever to stop the Lazy-L short of its destination. And, since horsebackers could make far better time than the slow-moving, ever-grazing herd, Rondeen might be lurking close by in spite of all the forced marches the Lazy-L had made.

And so the days became endless replicas of each other, the cattle streaming along, the continuous rumbling of their hooves an endless thunder, the wagons bobbing behind them, Stew Bidwell sitting stiffly on his seat, a rifle within easy reach, Consuelo and Jenny Rondeen likewise on guard. And that brief hour in the evening which belonged to the men became a subdued session wherein cowpokes spoke low-voiced, their eyes probing the prairie night.

Mitch still spent much of his spare time at Consuelo's wagon, and often during the day, when there were no recalcitrant cattle to haze back to the herd he would fall behind to ride alongside her, talking and laughing the while. By a dozen tokens he gave proof that he, too, was in love with Consuelo McQuade.

Under different circumstances, Chan might have pressed his own suit, for something within him rebelled at standing idly by while Mitch curried Consuelo's favor. But upon Chan's shoulders was a trail boss's responsibility, thrice multiplied now by the constant threat of a raid. His courting would have to wait until Whispering Basin was reached. And there — grim thought — there'd be little chance for any wooing, for he and Consuelo would then be out-and-out enemies, their truce of the trail a thing of the past.

Then there came a day when they dipped down the valley of the South Platte, another river was forded, and they were into Ogallala. Here Chan allowed his crew a brief holiday, compensation for the shortness of their stay in Dodge. And here, Jenny Rondeen contrived to sneak a gallon jug of whiskey into her wagon, for Chan saw her do it, though he said nothing about the matter. Futile had been his hope, he realized, that she might conquer her ancient weakness because of his wish. He had asked her not to drink on the trail. He could do no more.

Soon the longhorns were lumbering along again, pointed northward over more rolling country. Bluestem bunch grass stood almost stirrup-deep, a dry, rustling sea of it, proof that Nebraska had had a rainless summer. And it was here that disaster struck, suddenly and unexpectedly.

First there was a phantom of smoke, wafting upward over a distant rise, a hazy, nebulous blur along the northeast horizon. The steers stirred restlessly at the smell of it, showing signs of spooking, and all at once the smoke had become a billowing cloud, like a genie released from a bottle to grow to alarming proportions in a second's span. A breeze blew softly out of the northeast, the gentle push of it sending the smoke swirling down upon the drive.

"Prairie fire!" Billy Wing shouted excitedly from point position. "Hold the herd, boys. Don't let 'em get to stampeding."

This was an emergency that any Texan was trained to meet, for the arid plains of the Lone Star state had often known the devastating sweep of grass fires. With a sinister red line edging over the rise to creep down upon them, Chan and his crew went into action. Cutting a couple of steers out of the herd, Chan unleathered his gun, and, as the weapon spoke twice, the steers buckled at the knees and went down.

Other riders were doing the same swift sort of butchering, and Stew Bidwell, down off his chuck wagon, was coming on the run, a long knife in his hand. While Stew's knife was shuttling back and forth, disemboweling the dead steers, the riders were dropping ropes over the animals' horns, looping the lariats around their saddle horns.

"We passed an arroyo back a short piece," Chan barked at Billy Wing. "See if you can haze the herd into it. That way a couple of you can hold the beef, the rest can help fight the fire."

Then Chan was up into his saddle, the split carcass of a steer dragging behind him as he plunged out toward the fire which was moving down upon them all too fast. In his wake rode another rider, and another and another, each with a wet and grisly carcass at the end of his lass rope. Thus, by the most primitive of methods, they sought to blot out the fire. Within a hundred yards, each of those dead steers would be burned to a crisp, others brought up to take their place. But meanwhile those steers were like so many heavy, wet blankets, and they left smouldering, blackened ground in their bloody wake.

Riding parallel to the advancing fire, Chan caught a glimpse of a small group of riders over beyond the flames, and, even though that glimpse lasted for only a second, a swirling smoke pall blotting it out, Chan recognized the long, lean man who headed those horsemen. And now Chan knew that the fire hadn't sprung from the camp of some careless emigrant, or from any other accidental cause. This had been a set fire — and Caesar Rondeen had given it its start. For it was he who was yonder, along with part of his outfit.

A devilish scheme, Chan reflected angrily. With a fire to scare the steers into stampeding, the Lazy-L herd would be scattered from the North Platte to the Niobrara, and the crew, occupied in fighting the fire, wouldn't be able to check the stampede. Caesar Rondeen and his trail wolves could round up the longhorns at their leisure, or Rondeen could ride away and forget the matter, satisfied that the Lazy-L would have no herd to bring to Whispering. Thus, by a single stroke, Rondeen might bring ruin to the hopes of the Lorings.

But Rondeen wasn't going to get away with it, Chan decided. His high-boned face a taut mask of determination, he worked like a Trojan. Flames were leaping up around the hoofs of his horse, and the animal plunged in pain. The carcass that Chan had dragged slithering through the charring grass had served its purpose, and, turning back to get another, he discovered that Billy Wing had managed to maneuver the herd down into the coulee to the rear.

That gnarled little gnome of a man was doing an able job of holding the beef. Holy Joe Hawkins was helping him, and the coulee's walls penned in the bawling, frightened longhorns. The rest of the crew, freed for firefighting, was on foot, kicking out blazing tufts of grass. Ollie Archer extinguishing sparks with a shovel he'd gotten from the chuck wagon, Pete Still and Stew Bidwell busily butchering more steers.

It was hot work, work to sap a man's strength, and in that swirling inferno of smoke and flame Chan lost all track of time and effort, and it was as though the land itself were on fire, the universe a vast furnace or a multi-tongued beast that refused to be checked in its mad efforts to devour them. Heat and haze, boiling smoke and bawling steers, the stench of singed fetlocks and the snorting of wild-eyed horses — all these things blended into a weird pattern set against the lurid background of the creeping flames.

Were they fools to pit their puny efforts against this holocaust, Chan began to wonder? They might have started a backfire, but there'd been no time for such a try. Maybe it would be better to turn the herd to the south, he reasoned, and ride the stampede when the steers bolted. Thus they might save themselves, even though they lost precious miles and hours. But in that moment of black despair, destiny took a hand.

At first Chan was unaware of the change that had come, for he was like a blind man, groping through a blackened world. Then Ollie Archer's voice rose, shrill and triumphant, and the portent of his words knifed through Chan's consciousness, bringing him alert. "The wind!" Ollie cried. "*The wind's shifted*. Look — the fire's moving away from us."

Chan pawed at his streaming eyes. It was true. The prairie breeze, capricious as always, had turned, and was blowing out of the south. The fire that had been inching toward them in spite of all their efforts was now slowly retreating, the blackened swath of ground between the blaze and the Lazy-L crew growing wider with each passing moment. As the fire had advanced upon the Lazy-L, it had left a burned-out strip in its wake, but grass tufts had continued burning in that strip, and, as the wind veered, the flames bridged across the strip. And the next time the smoke pall parted, Chan saw Rondeen and his men in wild retreat before the marching flames. Like Franken-stein, Rondeen had created a monster which was now turning upon him.

It was a moment when a man might have given voice to joyful profanity or fallen on his knees in thankfulness — whichever his nature dictated. But Chan did neither, for, with good fortune smiling upon the Lazy-L, he was suddenly aware of a new calamity, the sight of it casting a chill upon him.

The chuck wagon and Jenny Rondeen's wagon had both been moved to the mouth of the coulee that now sheltered the herd. Stew Bidwell, busy with his butcher knife, had long since deserted the chuck wagon, and Consuelo had moved to the seat of it and was holding the rearing horses in check. Jenny Rondeen had been doing the same chore on her own wagon, but her horses had gotten out of hand. And now they were bolting wildly, racing straight toward that retreating wall of flame.

This much Chan saw in a glance, and horror took the heart out of him. He'd seen horses panicked by fire before. He'd seen them led blindfolded from a blazing stable only to turn and run back into the fire once the blindfolds were removed. And a like madness possessed the team that was dragging Jenny Rondeen to her doom.

Then Chan was racing after the wagon, and his grim prayer was that his cayuse, weary from fire-fighting, would be able to overtake it in time. Another rider was cutting in hot pursuit, too, riding at an angle from Chan, and he recognized the smokebegrimed features of Mitch. There was a stretch of space between them and Jenny Rondeen, a second stretch between her and the fire, and a great fear rose within Chan because she had the shortest distance to cover.

Mitch reached the wagon first. Racing alongside the fear-crazed team, he catapulted himself from the saddle onto the back of one of the runaway horses. There he clung, tugging desperately at the bit, striving to swerve the team. But still it raced onward, and Chan's new fear was that Mitch would be spilled from his precarious perch to fall beneath the wagon's wheels.

But Chan was abreast of the wagon now. He had a glimpse of Jenny Rondeen, her face gray with terror, the reins hanging laxly in her hands as though fear had paralyzed her. Then Chan swung from his own saddle to the seat beside her, seizing the reins and sawing frantically upon them.

Mitch had managed to whip off his neckerchief, and he was working valiantly to bind it about the eyes of the second horse. They were almost into that wall of flames as he succeeded, and at the same time Mitch threw his arm around the eyes of the horse he straddled. Up until now the team had paid no heed to Chan's frantic efforts to check them, but, blinded, they responded instinctively to his guidance. A blast of heat smote them as Chan swung the wagon around, and he wondered if the canvas top would catch afire. Then they were heading back out of danger, and, as the wagon slowed down, Mitch slipped safely to the ground.

"God," Whiskey Jenny said tonelessly, a woman released from a trance. "Now I owe my *life* to a Loring."

"It took a lot of nerve and some quick thinking to do what Mitch did," Chan said fervently. "We owe him plenty — both of us."

They were back among the waiting crew, and the wagon came to a halt, Consuelo flying to Jenny's side, the men surging forward to pump the hands of Chan and Mitch, and there was a great deal of back-slapping and profane praise. But congratulations had to be brief, for there was work to be done. Stew Bidwell was doling out lard from the chuck wagon, and the crew busily applied it to the singed fetlocks of the valiant cayuses who had helped fight the fire.

"Seeing as the herd's quieted down some, let's get them to moving," Chan suggested to Billy Wing as the two studied the retreating fire which would undoubtedly rage until it reached some creek bank and burned itself out. "This is one time Caesar Rondeen built himself a boomerang. So long as the fire is between him and us, we won't have to worry."

And so the herd was put on the move again, and several of the crew were sent to help Ollie Archer round up the remuda which had bolted, and when sunset came there was only a red, faraway glow against the sky to remind them of the peril they had fought this day. But the episode had its sequel, and it came when Chan heard his name called from the direction of Jenny Rondeen's wagon after the herd had been bedded down that evening.

"I've thanked Mitch," Jenny Rondeen said when he came to her. "And I've been waiting for a chance to thank you, Chan. You were brave, mighty brave, both of you."

"Mother —" he said, and ran out of words.

She shoved a straggly wisp of hair from her eyes with a trembling hand, and he realized, with a start, that she'd been crying.

"There were twenty years when I thought that I'd rather be dead than living," she said.

"But today, when death was so near, I knew that I didn't really feel that way about it, that I wanted desperately to live. And then, when I'd lost all hope, the two of you came riding . . . Thank you — son."

Seeing the shape of opportunity, Chan seized it eagerly. "If you're beholdin' to me for what I did, there's a way you can prove it," he said. "I've hoped that you'd quit drinking, mother. Like I told you back in Texas, it would please me mightily if you did."

She made no answer, and there was nothing more to be said, but as he turned away he had the feeling that speech was trembling on her lips. He was back to his blankets when he heard a crash as something was shattered against wagon hub yonder in the darkness. He knew then that Jenny Rondeen had smashed the jug of whiskey she'd fetched from Ogallala. And he also knew, somehow, that Jenny Rondeen had taken her last drink.

Smiling, he went to sleep.

Chapter Fifteen

Now the Niobrara was behind them, and they were into the southwestern corner of the Dakotas, the land of the Black Hills, once upon a time the *Pah Sappa* of the Sioux, and the flatness of the prairie was a memory belonging to the yesterdays in this majestic land of pine-blackened upthrusts.

From the mouth of the Niobrara north of Milk River had been Sioux country in the days when the steam packets had flourished on the Missouri, the whole north country a vast wilderness throbbing to restless war drums. But after the Custer massacre, the might of the United States Army had been hurled against Sitting Bull, forcing him to flee across the Canadian line. Now that able medicine man was back, living along the Grand River in North Dakota, so the tale was told, and Ogallala had been rife with rumors that the Sioux danced their ghost dance and Sitting Bull made talk of another outbreak against the whites.

So another menace hovered beyond the horizon to harass the Lazy-L, but at least the threat of this new danger gave a respite from the old one. There'd been no sign of Caesar Rondeen since the day of the prairie fire, and Chan had kept a wary eye for a second fire since Rondeen might reason that what had almost succeeded once would surely succeed with another try. But the Lazy-L drive was now well west of the ninety-eighth meridian, and consequently, deep into short grass country where a fire would not be so devastating. And Chan was about convinced that Caesar Rondeen had gone on ahead, being not at all anxious to linger in the land of the Sioux.

But still the trail smiled, and the Cheyenne had been crossed, the drive skirting notorious Deadwood, fording the Belle Fourche and pressing onward until the day of days came. Chan, riding point position, had begun to recognize landmarks, and on a certain afternoon he beckoned to Billy Wing and swept his arm to the northwest.

"Montana," Chan said simply. "We crossed out of Dakota this morning, I'm thinking. A few days more will find us at Fort Faraday on the Yellowstone. Another week or so, and Lazy-L cattle will be grazing in Whispering."

His words went from mouth to mouth, flankers calling the news to drag men, drag men shouting it back to the wagons, and a new surge of spirit came to the Lazy-L, even the longhorns plodding along as though they realized that the end of the thundering trail was not far beyond. But to Chan there was a nameless sadness because most of the miles now lay behind them. Whispering meant showdown, and the trail had been a reprieve from the inevitable.

He took the early watch that evening, as was his custom, and when he rode in and roused the men of the second nighthawking shift, he would have sought his blankets, except that it was then Consuelo called to him from her wagon, her voice soft and plaintive.

They were into prairie country again, and the moon was just beginning to nudge over the eastern rim of the land, and at first the girl was hazy and spectral in the gloom. She was standing beside the wagon she shared with Jenny Rondeen, and he was almost upon her before he realized what had wrought the transformation in her tonight.

Always she'd worn riding garb, in Whispering, and in Texas, and on the trail between. But tonight she'd donned a flowing white dress, frilly and ethereal, drawn in at the waist by a flaring blue sash. Her bare shoulders and arms were like old ivory, and she made a picture that took Chan's breath away, carrying him in memory back to old San Antonio with its pillared mansions and the grand ladies who promenaded before them.

"Consuelo," he said softly. "You're beautiful!"

"You like this?" She smiled and curtsied, then spun slowly about on her heel. "I buy it in Ogallala, and tonight is the first time I wear it."

She was so elfin, so much like a little girl showing off, and at the same time she was so utterly desirable that his blood pounded in his temples, and the hunger that had been his across the miles threatened to overpower him. Yet he held himself in check, standing there awkwardly.

"You never come to talk to me, Chan," she complained. "Always it is Mitch who keeps me from being lonely. Why is that, Chan?"

"Well now," he grinned, "I haven't got so many sombreroes that I can afford to have you shoot holes in all of them. Besides, I've been right busy. But it's a nice night, and I could sort of make up for my shortcomings. Shall we sit on the wagon seat?"

She held a finger to her lips. "The *Señora* Rondeen is sleeping," she cautioned. "Poor thing, the trail is long and hard for her."

He gave her his arm, and they strolled out across the prairie until they came to a large, flat rock, broad enough to accommodate the two of them. "You've been good company for her," Chan said, jerking his thumb toward the

177

wagon. "I want to thank you for coming along with us."

"She is a woman who has suffered much, this *madre* of yours. You are surprised, Chan? Oh yes, I know all the story, for she tell me about it on the trail — the great love she has for the caballero, Slade Rondeen, who is your father, and the bitterness that comes to her when he is killed by King Loring. And she say how it twist her heart when her *niño* is take by King Loring to raise."

"I know," Chan said thoughtfully. "I can understand her bitterness, and I've hoped that I could make it up to her for the black years. But we've been like strangers, she and I, except for once — the night after the prairie fire. I'd thought that the trail might bring us closer together, but I've had little chance to spend time with her."

"To her, it must be like finding something she had lost for a long time," Consuelo reflected. "But the *niño* has become a man, and the gap between is great. But hers is the heart of a mother, Chan. And there will come a day when it will call aloud and you will hear it. I know. I have seen her eyes when she watch you and Mitch from her wagon seat. And you remember the night when we go into Dodge City — the time you are afraid I will tell the law that the Triangle is the outfit they are looking for? The *señora* Rondeen did not know I have told you I do not use the law in our fight. She was worry' for fear I give you away, and she make me bring the wagon back out to the herd, instead of staying in the nice hotel that night."

But Chan was scarcely listening, for a sudden suspicion had touched him at the mention of Mitch's name. "Mitch?" he asked. "He hasn't any idea what Jenny Rondeen is to me?"

Her eyes widened with surprise. "He knows the truth," was her startling reply. "He has been at our wagon when the *señora* has talk with me."

So Mitch knew that Chan Loring was in reality a Rondeen. Chan fell silent, pondering the strangeness of Mitch Loring who'd come into possession of the very secret Billy Wing had wanted kept from the King's son, yet who'd never given any sign that he had such knowledge. But was that the reason Mitch deliberately nursed a grudge against him, Chan wondered? Did Mitch hate him solely because he was a Rondeen? But there was no answer, and Consuelo was speaking again.

"Soon we see Whispering?" she ventured.

"Yes," he said and knew that the inevitable must be faced. "What then, Consuelo?"

Her shrug was wholly Latin. "What then?" she repeated. "*Quien sabe?* Who knows? You

179

have the homestead papers to claim Whispering. You will use those papers, Chan?"

"I don't know," he said. "The King's will was never read, Consuelo. Billy Wing packs it, and he'll show it to us at trail's end. I expect it will name Mitch boss of the Lazy-L. What happens then will be up to him. But I reckon it won't make much difference, anyway. The King wanted Whispering, and either one of us will fight to do things the King's way. Yet the basin is big enough for everybody. If Angus McQuade could meet us halfway —"

"He is one hard *hombre*, my *padre*," Consuelo said. "But in him is one soft heart. You see, he has got a code, this Angus McQuade. Long time ago he is a Confederate soldier, but after Appomattox he do not surrender. Instead he take ten-twelve friends, Texas men, and go down into Mexico. That is where he meet my *madre*, and I am born."

She paused, gazing back across the years, and Chan waited in respectful silence. "It is hard business, the building of ranches in Mexico," Consuelo went on. "We are living in Chihauhua, and the fierce, wild Yaquis come to kill and burn. But always my *padre* and his friends make the fight, and always they stick. But after the Yaquis are chased into the hills, there comes a new kind of fight that is too big for even Angus McQuade to win."

"A revolution?" Chan guessed.

"A braggart in gold braid and shiny boots who calls himself the emancipator of all *Mejico* is come," she said. "He wins much power, but he use it to make the lot of the peons worse than before. Him Angus McQuade and his friends fight, but this braggart has got many guns and many followers. Soon it is flee or die, so Angus McQuade make the big move once again, turning his back on the grave of my mother, and herding his cattle north to the land he never forgot. That is how Angus McQuade come back to Whispering."

"I see," Chan said, and fell silent, visualizing those bitter years when a stubborn Texan had tried to carve out a place for himself against insurmountable odds, sensing how those years had made their mark upon the man. "Then Angus McQuade is making his last ditch stand in Whispering."

"He is too old to always go looking for the place where he can stay," she said. "And it is the code of the McQuades to fight for what they want. Always it has been that way. It must be that way in Whispering."

"Then I'll say this," Chan said slowly. "If it is for me to help decide, and there's a way that things can be settled peaceable, I'll take that way. But if that can not be, then there'll have to be war, Consuelo."

181

"The answer is good enough for me," she said. "It is a promise?"

"A promise," he agreed.

"Then we seal it," she said, and her arms slipped around his neck, her lips coming to meet his, and a thousand promises might have been sealed by such a kiss.

"Good night," he finally said hoarsely, fetching himself back to reality by sheer force of will, and stumbling away, knowing that to tarry longer might take the last of his strength away from him, and that other promises might follow — promises he'd never be able to keep.

There was a singing elation within him as he tumbled into his blankets, and for a long time sleep wouldn't come. He awoke feeling strangely happy, though the episode of the night before was like something borrowed from a dream. Thus he went directly to Consuelo's wagon, calling her name softly, knowing that the sight of her would restore the lost magic of the night before. And he wanted to tell her that between them they would find a way out of the trouble that loomed ahead.

But only the sleepy voice of Jenny Rondeen answered his call. "Consuelo isn't here," the woman insisted, and at first her reply made no sense. Then the truth dawned upon Chan. Consuelo had vanished in the night.

Chapter Sixteen

Because Caesar Rondeen had been at the bottom of most of the misfortunes that had befallen the Lazy-L, Chan's instant suspicion was that Rondeen had had something to do with Consuelo's nocturnal disappearance. Thus Chan was a man berserk with fear and rage in that first awful minute of discovery, his startled shouts fetching the rest of the crew on the run. Jenny Rondeen came clambering out of the wagon, a robe thrown hastily around her shoulders, and the air sizzled with everyone's barked questions.

"Wait!" Ollie Archer, the kid wrangler, quavered. "If she was kidnapped, it weren't here at the camp. She came out to the remuda last night after midnight and got her own saddler. Said she couldn't sleep and wanted to take a little ride in the moonlight. I argued ag'in it, seeing as this is dangerous country in more ways than one. But she had her mind set on ridin', she did."

"I heard her stirring about," Stew Bidwell put in. "Fact is, I woke up and found her near the chuck wagon. But I didn't figger —"

Now a new suspicion had taken hold of Chan, and he clambered into the chuck wagon, fumbling about for the strong box that contained the Lazy-L's money and the homestead entry papers. He'd opened that box twice on the trail — once in Dodge City when he'd doled out wages to his crew, and again in Ogallala when some of his hands had drawn money. Consuelo hadn't been around on the first occasion, but she'd seen him unlock the box in Nebraska. And she knew that he carried its key in his shirt pocket.

Reaching for the box now, Chan also reached for the key. But the key wasn't in his pocket; it was protruding from the lock. And even before he opened the box, he knew all its contents would be intact save for the homestead entry papers.

Climbing out of the chuck wagon, he faced his crew and made frank confession. "She's gone on to Whispering," he said. "And she's got the papers that give us legal claim to the Basin. She managed to get the key away from me last night, though I didn't know it at the time."

His jaw tightened as he saw the grin on Mitch's face. "There's nothing for us to do but go on," Chan added. "Those papers may not do her much good, since there's copies of 'em in the land agent's office — but that's

184

a long ways off, and in the wrong direction. But that makes no never mind. If we can't take Whispering one way, we can shore take it another."

Now he knew why she'd kissed him, and he cursed himself for his blindness, knowing her nimble fingers had been at work in the unguarded moment when she'd been in his arms. But the very manner by which she'd accomplished her coup gave him a determination to wrest the Basin from her and her people. Thus anger eased some of the ache that grew within him at the thought that her kiss had been a mockery without real meaning.

He might have taken her trail alone, hoping to catch up with her and force the entry papers from her before she reached Whispering with them. But this was Consuelo's country, and she'd know every mile of it. Scant chance of outfoxing her under the circumstances. So he rode grim and silent that day, pointing the herd to the north and west, until they drank from the Yellowstone in mid-afternoon, skirting that historic stream in the ensuing hours until darkness overtook them.

They were on with the dawn, veering south and west now, following the windings of the Yellowstone, and sometimes looking down from rimrock upthrusts to see the river meandering below them. And the next day, near noon, they saw a palisaded huddle of buildings ahead, the Stars and Stripes fluttering in the breeze high above the parade ground, and no man needed to be told that yonder sprawled Fort Faraday.

Before the fort, Chan signalled the hands to mill the herd, and then the crew was given the chore of cutting out the four-year-olds that would become soldier beef, separating them from the younger beef and the she-stuff that would stock the Lazy-L's new spread when they reached Whispering.

While this was being done, Chan and Mitch and Billy Wing rode to the fort, where a pacing sentry presented arms and let them pass. Riding across the parade ground, they swung from saddles before the commanding officer's headquarters, there to be greeted by a tall, bronzed officer whose shoulder straps bore the gold oak-leaves on yellow of a cavalry Major. Chan had met him before when he'd made his dicker to provide Texas beef, and the two shook hands heartily.

"My brother, Mitchell Loring, Major Ransome, and our *segundo,* Billy Wing," Chan said. "If you'd like to inspect the herd, it will be ready shortly."

Soon the four of them rode back to the herd, Major Ransome urging his horse into the midst of the longhorns, crossing and recrossing the herd until the blue of his uniform and the yellow stripe along his leg became one beneath the gray mantle of dust. When he finally rode back to the Lorings, Major Ransome smiled.

"Fine beef, gentlemen," he said. "Considering the distance you've had to cover, its condition is in itself a compliment to your ability as trail men. I accept it without question, and if you'll come back to my office, I shall prepare a voucher for you at once."

Riding back, Chan asked. "You haven't seen anything of a one-eyed man hereabouts, Major? I'm referring to a Texan who might have headed this way with a party of men in the past two weeks or so."

"A one-eyed man? He came through here a week or ten days ago and headed on toward the Whispering country. Had twenty or thirty men with him, and a half dozen wagons. I'd have thought they were a homesteading outfit if it hadn't been for the absence of women and children and the fact that they were as hard-looking as I've seen for quite some time."

Chan whistled softly. Truly, Caesar Rondeen had gathered strength since leaving Dodge City, and the fact that Rondeen was at least a week ahead of the Lazy-L bore out Chan's theory that the man had chosen to forge onward rather than tarry on the trail.

Major Ransome extended the voucher. "You're pushing on to Whispering with the rest of your herd, I understand. But you must be weary, you and your men. If you'd care to rest up here at the fort for a couple of days, we'd be glad to have you as our guests."

"No, thanks," Chan replied. "We'll be getting along, Major."

For now he was more anxious than ever to reach the end of the trail. Caesar Rondeen was ahead, and no knowing what manner of deviltry the man might be brewing. They must allow Rondeen no more time to prepare himself than necessary. And so, before that day was finished, the Lazy-L was on the move again, half-a-herd now, two thousand longhorns instead of four thousand. But Chan was retaining his full crew, for they'd be needed on the ranch in Whispering.

They forded the Yellowstone just above the point where the Whispering emptied into the greater river, then skirted the Whispering, veering almost directly north and to the west, and with the passing days the country underwent a change. Gone was the flatness of the prairieland, for the terrain was rough and broken now, and a smear of hills lay against the horizon, old and mighty and mysterious.

A wild land, this Whispering range, and, nearing the Basin, Chan thought of the girl who called this country home. He was supposed to hate her now. Yet the heart of him couldn't accept the lie, and he wondered where she was and how she'd fared across the miles since she'd left the herd. And because Caesar Rondeen was somewhere ahead, he knew the gnaw of worry. Yet Consuelo McQuade was no fragile flower who might wither before the first blast of trouble. That Chan knew. She could take care of herself — all too well, Chan reflected ruefully.

Another day found them threading a valley, and because Chan knew this valley was Whispering Pass, a lesser valley leading into a greater one, he also knew that trail's end was near. The river had narrowed considerably now, and there was timber on the slopes on either hand, the dark blue of evergreen stretching above and beyond the brown of buckbrush. And as they proceeded, the Pass narrowed, the hills on either side seeming to rise straight up until their timberfringed crowns were lost in the smiling reaches of the sky.

"Thunder on the Pecos," Billy Wing observed. "Half-a-dozen jiggers with as many rifles could hunker down in the timber and hold this Pass ag'in all the sojers from Fort Faraday, if needs be. A fine place this would be for somebody to have a bushwhackin' party."

"That's right," Chan agreed absently, and knew that for him a moment had come that could no longer be delayed. If there had to be a series of showdowns, this was the place for the first.

He lifted his arm in the sweeping, circular motion that was a signal to mill the herd, his amazed riders obeying him, forcing the point of the arrowhead back upon itself and finally bringing the cattle to a standstill. Whereupon Chan motioned for the crew to gather around him, and when they did he sat his saddle for a long moment, eyeing these men who'd followed him from Texas.

"We've reached Whispering," Chan announced then. "Another mile or two, and this valley broadens out and becomes the Basin. And here's where you get a new boss, boys."

A murmur swept through the huddled men, and he let it have its way. "Back in Texas, King Loring gave me two orders the night he died," Chan went on. "One was to bring the herd to Whispering — and that one I've just fulfilled."

His eyes flicked to Mitch, who sat nearby, patently puzzled as to what Chan intended to say.

"You, Mitch, you disputed my right to be trail boss, and we fought to see if things would be done as the King asked or not. I won that fight, and I'll say that you played your end of it square, taking orders like the rest of the hands. Which is one reason that I've known all along that I'd have to play just as square when the time came."

Again his gaze drifted to the crew. "I reckon all of you knew I was no blood kin to the King," he said. "The story went that I was a wagon-train orphan. Before I left Texas I learned that that story wasn't true. My name is Rondeen, boys. Yes, I'm Slade Rondeen's son, and the King took me to raise because he felt he owed me that much after downing my dad. That's why Jenny Rondeen is along with us. She's my mother, and it was the King's wish, as well as mine, that she be taken care of. But because I'm a Rondeen, I know I haven't any real claim whatsoever to be bossing the Lazy-L. It belongs to King Loring's kid, and he's boss from here on out."

He glanced at Mitch once more. "You made your say back in the Nations about what would happen to me the day we reached Whispering, Mitch. That day has come. There's no denying that you're the only one with rightful claim to the Lazy-L. For myself, I'm asking nothing. For my mother, I'm asking the same consideration the King gave her.

"There'll be a fight on ahead — a three-sided fight. I think I proved back in Dodge,

Mitch, that I don't play Caesar Rondeen's game and that in spite of our blood tie, I'm backing the Lazy-L against him. If it came to an out-and-out showdown where it was my gun against Rondeen's, I'd probably back down. Blood *is* thicker than water. But I'm staying if you'll have me. What do you say, Mitch?"

His announcement had been a bombshell, a great surprise to everyone here save Billy Wing, Jenny Rondeen, and Mitch himself, who'd known Chan's true identity all along. Yet Mitch's eyes held as much astonishment as anyone's — but for a different reason, Chan knew. Mitch hadn't expected to find the cards faced in such a manner.

And now Mitch would have to speak, and all of Chan's hopes hung on the answer, but before Mitch could find words, Billy Wing barked out, "Look!" and pointed northward up the valley. "Thunder on the Pecos, if it ain't trouble comin' bearin' a flag o' truce."

His words swung every eye in the direction he'd indicated, and there, riding along, came five horsebackers, the one in the lead filling a saddle to overflowing, a big, red-faced, red-whiskered giant who bore a white flag which was tied, suggestively enough, to a rifle-barrel. And because Chan was the only one who'd ever seen him before, it was Chan who gasped,

"Angus McQuade."

Loping into speaking distance, McQuade reined his horse to a halt, his companions following suit, the ex-Confederate who'd never surrendered surveying the grouped Texans with his fierce, old eyes, a man adamant.

"I've not come to waste wor-rds with ye Lor-rings," he snapped. "Ye'll go no further, understand. Tis a deadline I'm placing for ye, just as I've set one for that son of satan, Caesar R-rondeen. The Pass is guarded, do ye ken? Try to go on, and it's hot lead ye'll stop. And it's the gun of every mon in Whisper-ring that's backing me."

But Chan Loring was paying him scant heed, just as he was also ignoring the three men who sat their saddles behind McQuade — other ranchers of Whispering, doubtless, men who'd followed the fiery Scotchman from the Lone Star to Old Mexico and then up to Montana. For Consuelo McQuade was with her father. And there was scorn in Chan's eyes as he faced her once again.

193

Chapter Seventeen

Angus McQuade had made his say, and already he was whirling his horse about, his silent friends following suit, but still Consuelo sat her saddle, her eyes locked with Chan's.

"Come along, lass," her father ordered. "We'll no want to be tarryin' here."

"I'll catch up with you," she promised. "Me, I have the things to say, too. And do not worry, *padre*. These gringoes are not such bad *hombres* like the *Señor* Rondeen."

With a massive shrug, Angus McQuade touched steel to his cayuse and went his way, and Consuelo still stared at Chan. When she did speak, it was though the two of them were alone in this vast, hill-hemmed land, though the Lazy-L crew still clustered about in that same stupefied silence.

"You are very angry with me, Chan," she said. "You think I am the *ladron*, the thief who steal your homestead papers and run away. It is true. Yet is this a worse thing I do than when you file the papers after my *padre* and his *amigos* are already settled in Whispering Basin? Always we have know

194

there must be a fight between us in Whispering, you and me. I was jus' shoot the first gun."

"Fair enough!" Chan snapped. "The pot can't call the kettle black. But —" He glanced about, wishing mightily that his staring crew was elsewhere. "That night on the rock when we talked things over — I thought — But what difference does it make?"

"You think eyerything I do is the lie," she flared up. "*Por Dios,* if I do not come ahead to Whispering, Angus McQuade would have met you with the rifle, but there would have been no white flag tied to it. It is because I learn to like you and Mitch and *Señora* Rondeen and the others on the trail that I am come on here to tell my *padre* that he should give you the chance before shooting."

"Well, he certainly told us how he stands all right," Chan conceded hotly. "And as long as he's got the guns to hold the Pass, I reckon he has a fistful of aces. But he can't hold out forever. We're camping right here for a spell, and be damned to his deadline. And you can tell him so!"

She shrugged, a gesture embodying both defiance and hopelessness, and glanced at Jenny Rondeen, who sat upon her wagon seat listening to all this in stony silence.

"In the basin we have a settlement, the town

of Whispering," Consuelo said. "Soon now there comes the fall rains, and it will not be nice out here in the Pass. If the *Señora* Rondeen wish to be my guest, she can come to Whispering with me. The trail has been long, and it will be good for her to sleep in a bed again."

There was so much of sincerity and consideration in that invitation that it almost melted the stone in Chan's heart. But at the same time, because part of his pride was still bruised, he hoped that Jenny Rondeen would scornfully refuse the offer. But Whiskey Jenny smiled and said, "Yes, I'll go along. Thank you, my dear."

Then, amazingly, she managed a wink in Chan's direction, and, seeing that gesture, Chan felt a sudden kinship between himself and the woman. It was as though Whiskey Jenny had said, "Why shouldn't I go with her? It's a chance for one of us to get inside the enemy's stronghold."

Consuelo hadn't seen the wink. Maneuvering her horse alongside Jenny's wagon, she stepped across to the seat and took the reins from the older woman's hands, handing Jenny the reins of the saddler to trail along. Then, without another glance at Chan, the girl clucked the horses into motion, the wagon slowly lumbering away, bobbing across the valley's floor until it finally blended with the distance and was gone.

Whereupon Chan sighed gustily, then remembered a showdown deferred, and turned to face it. "Well, Mitch?" he asked. "You never had a chance to give me my answer."

For a long moment Mitch didn't speak, and then he said haltingly, "Maybe because being top-hand was so important to me, I thought that you were always trying to outdo me. That's why I was riled when you declared yourself trail boss down in Texas. And when you clouted me off my horse down in the Territory, I thought you were just trying to show off your authority in front of Consuelo. Then, when I learned you were a Rondeen, I hated you more. Sure, I knew you weren't playing Caesar Rondeen's game. But I suspected you were after a stake of your own — the Lazy-L. But today you make the biggest damn' fool in Montana out of me."

"Meaning — ?" Chan invited.

"Meaning that you turned around and gave up the very thing I was sure you were after," Mitch blurted. "Meaning that you handed me the Lazy-L — and no argument about it. Chan —" His hand went out hesitantly. "If you can see your way clear to take half-a-step . . . ."

"I'd come further than that," Chan choked,

and took the proferred hand. "I reckon we understand each other now, Mitch. Maybe for the first time in our lives. There's much we both might say, but we'll let that pass. Right now our chore is to figger the way to get this outfit into Whispering."

"You got any idea?" Mitch asked humbly. "As far as I'm concerned, if it was for me to say, I'd be for sharing the basin with the McQuade outfit. There's room enough for all of us, according to what Consuelo's told me when we talked on the trail. But it looks like old Angus isn't interested in a compromise, and since we've lost the entry papers we can't make him an offer."

Had Mitch's decision to share the basin been born of those nights when he'd kept Consuelo company at her wagon, Chan wondered? But he said nothing about that, for their common interest in Consuelo was the one difference that hadn't been dissolved between them, and he had no wish to sully their new understanding by mentioning it.

Instead he said, "Come dark, maybe we can take a little *pasear* beyond the rifles that are holding the Pass and have a look-see at the lay of the land."

Thus it was decided, and the rest of the day was in the nature of a holiday for the crew, since it took very little effort to hold the herd at this point, and there was the luxury of hours on end with nothing to do but loaf. But with the sun dipping behind the western wall of the Pass, Mitch, who'd been sprawling beside the chuck wagon, came hastily to his feet, pointing.

"Flags of truce must be the fashion in Whispering Basin," he observed. "Here comes another gent waving a white rag."

"Yes," Chan agreed. "But I never expected to see Doc Menafee packing one."

For it was indeed Caesar Rondeen's gunhawk who came now, reining to a halt as he drew nearer. Chan hadn't seen the man since that night in Dodge City when he, Chan, had plucked Mitch out of Rondeen's hands and thereafter swapped lead with Menafee, Jube Cazborg, and the kingpin himself. Now Menafee sat his saddle, his lips skinned back from his yellowish teeth in what was apparently meant to pass for a smile, the man acutely ill at ease the presence of the Lazy-L.

"Well, spill it." Chan urged. "What fetches you here besides your horse, Menafee?"

"Loring, the boss wants to see you," Menafee said. "He says he'll give you his solemn word that not a cap will be cracked before and after the palaver. If you'll come along, I'll take you to him."

"There's nothing," Chan said flatly, "that

I want to say to Caesar Rondeen."

"You galoots want to get hold of Whispering Basin, don't you?" Menafee countered. "How you gonna, so long as McQuade is top-hand? Maybe the boss wants to talk about joinin' forces for a spell?"

"Nothing doing," Chan said.

"It ain't gonna hurt to come talk to the boss," Menafee sneered. "What's the matter, feller? Afraid to get out of sight of these boys of your'n?"

From the corner of his mouth Chan said, "Catch up my cayuse, Ollie, and slap a kak on it."

"This smells like a trap to me," Billy Wing spoke up. "Don't let this gun-totin' skeleton talk you into anything, Chan."

"Don't worry," Chan said, and eyed the stringy length of Doc Menafee significantly. "If it turns out to be a trap, at least one varmint will lose his hide. And I reckon that not even Caesar Rondeen would dishonor a flag of truce."

Thus it came about that he rode up the valley with Doc Menafee, for Chan had surrendered to a consuming curiosity as to why Caesar Rondeen had sent for him. And with the purple shadows shuttling down the slopes, they came at last to a place where a sizable camp had been. This might have been

200

Rondeen's stopping place once, but Doc Menafee only grinned at Chan as they passed it.

Then the Pass widened, and they were into Whispering Basin itself, and still no one had challenged them, though Angus McQuade had claimed the Pass was guarded. A scatteration of buildings loomed ahead in the last light of the day — the town of Whispering — and because this was McQuade territory, according to what Consuelo had said, Chan wondered just where Angus McQuade had established his deadline for Caesar Rondeen.

"The boss is in yonder town," Doc Menafee admitted. "Now don't go askin' me why McQuade rifles didn't stop him. He'll tell you all you need to know."

Whispering Town had been no more than a log community hall when Chan had been here before, but from such a start, a sizable settlement had grown in the intervening months. Probably far-sighted traders, gambling that the Basin would flourish in the future, had come here with Angus McQuade's permission, building a town to serve the new range. In any event, Whispering was big enough to have a single straggly street, two rows of false-fronted buildings facing each other across a dust-churned thoroughfare.

A long line of canvas-topped wagons stood

along the street, and some of these wagons Chan had seen before. Caesar Rondeen was in Whispering, no doubt about that, and when the two dismounted to tramp inside a two-story building, Chan gasped in surprise, for the furnishings of Rondeen's old Spur Wheel Saloon, transported by wagon, now decorated the interior of this log structure the breadth of a nation away from Rawson. Even the same cigarette-scarred piano was here, the same pasty-faced player huddled over it.

The men who lined the bar were not the men who'd followed Angus McQuade from Old Mexico, and it was more than instinct that told Chan that here was part of the crew of trail wolves who called Caesar Rondeen master. Their eyes measured Chan calculatingly, but he kept his own eyes ahead, treading on Menafee's heels up a crude stairway and into a room above. And there Doc Menafee left him, fading away down the stairs, and Chan stood facing Caesar Rondeen.

"So you've come, Chan," Rondeen said. "Have a chair, my boy. I'm more than glad to see you!"

"Are you?" Chan asked, and chose to stand. And here in this room with that one-eyed, blacked-garbed man seated behind the same desk as of yore, it was like that night in Rawson when he'd faced Rondeen above the Spur

Wheel. "What is it you've got to say, Rondeen?"

The man spread his hands wearily. "Where shall I begin?" he asked. "All that I have to say, I've said before. But I wanted to offer you a last chance, Chan. Throw in with me, boy. Ah, you doubt the sincerity of my offer. You're remembering the little incident in the camp of the Comanches when there was talk of turning you over to Jube's mercies. That little feud between you and Jube is personal, and no affair of mine. And you'd struck me, Chan, remember? In the heat of your anger, you'd forgotten our blood tie, and I forgot as well. But that tie remains. That's why I want you on my side."

"And I'm still not interested," Chan snapped. "I don't know how you've gotten this far into Whispering. Maybe Angus allowed you this much leeway. But regardless, you've no better chance of taking Whispering than I have. And I'm not teaming up with you."

Rondeen shrugged. "And that is where you're making a mistake," he said soothingly. "You think McQuade will stop me, eh? A seasoned campaigner, old Angus. Consider how strategically he arranged to guard the Pass. But did riflemen stop you when you came through with Doc? No, Chan. Angus

McQuade had the means to hold this Basin against the legions of hell, if necessary, but all of his planning was undone in a moment. Achilles had his heel, and Angus McQuade had his one vulnerable spot as well.

"Perhaps Doc gave you the impression that I was interested in an alliance with the Lazy-L in order to beat McQuade. That was to toll you here so I could talk to you. Actually, Whispering is in my hand. But it would be nice to have the Lazy-L longhorns to stock it. I told you once that I have the means of making you master of the Lazy-L. Think, Chan! You and I — one Rondeen and another — masters here. Down in hell, Slade Rondeen could laugh in the face of King Loring."

It came to Chan, then, that there was sincerity in the single eye of Caesar Rondeen, and that the tie between them did mean something to the man in spite of their enmity of the trail. And it was a moment when Chan might have been sorely tempted. Up until today, there'd been nothing at trail's end for him. But because Mitch had given him his hand, all things had changed.

"There's nothing between us but our blood — and I'm not responsible for that," Chan said. "We could never pull together, Rondeen. You've had your say, and I've heard you out. Now I'm leaving."

Then he was marching down the stairs, crossing the barroom, his back muscles stiffened against the impact of lead, for here was the true test of the worth of Caesar Rondeen's flag of truce. And Jube Cazborg, for instance, would pay no heed to anything as flimsy as a promise. But Cazborg was nowhere around. Stepping up into his saddle. Chan took a quick turn up and down the street, then bee-lined back toward the Lazy-L herd.

Jenny Rondeen's wagon wasn't in Whispering. Which meant that Consuelo had taken her guest on to the McQuade ranch, doubtless. Chan breathed easier for that. Certainly Rondeen ruled the town of Whispering, yet Chan put little credence in the man's claim that he also held the Basin in the palm of his hand. That had been bluff talk, an added inducement for Chan to throw in with him. But the shape of showdown was looming larger. Chan had been given his last chance, and had turned it down. Maybe Rondeen would strike at the herd now, waging his bitter war against both the Lorings and the McQuades.

And so Chan Loring, riding with a thousand questions and doubts to puzzle him, came back to the bedded herd, there to find a wildly excited Billy Wing awaiting him.

"Chan," the old man shouted. "You've got

to go after Mitch."

"Mitch?"

"He got to frettin' about you after you left, fearin' maybe that Rondeen had tolled you into a trap. So Mitch saddled up and lit out toward the Basin. He run into some of McQuade's friends and got the news, so he lit a shuck back here, ordered me to keep every hand watchin' the herd. McQuade turned Whispering Town over to Rondeen this afternoon, and now Mitch is afraid Rondeen's gonna strike at us."

"McQuade turned the town over to Rondeen," Chan gasped. "Rondeen claimed he had Whispering when I talked to him today — but I thought he was bluffing. But why did McQuade do it?"

"Some of Rondeen's men grabbed Consuelo and your maw after they left here with the wagon this morning," Billy hastily explained. "Don't ask me how they managed to do it in spite of McQuade's guards! Rondeen's holding 'em prisoners somewhere, and he ain't lettin' the girl go until McQuade and his friends move outa Whispering. And Mitch took the trail alone to try and save Consuelo. Thunder on the Pecos, Chan, if —"

But Chan was already wheeling his horse, pointing the mount to the north again. For now Chan knew what Caesar Rondeen had meant by Angus McQuade's vulnerable spot. And Chan also knew that three people who meant the world to him were in grave danger.

There was work for a fighting man tonight.

Chapter Eighteen

Tooling Jenny Rondeen's wagon up out of Whispering Pass, Consuelo McQuade had been exceedingly quiet, for she was deep in thought, and though twin spots of color on her cheeks evidenced that anger stirred her, there was, at the same time, a brooding sadness in her dark eyes. Her bitter exchange of words with Chan Loring was still fresh in her mind and once she said, with forced rancor, "Stubborn gringo pig."

The Lazy-L herd was well behind the wagon, and now the pass was broadening out, and to Consuelo's right lay the camp that Caesar Rondeen had maintained since he'd come to Whispering a week or so before. But Consuelo drove past the huddle of tents and wagons with haughty indifference, for yonder, in the brush that covered the left side of the Pass, a dozen guards had been posted by her father to keep a watchful eye on Rondeen's outfit — and on the other interlopers who'd today come to Whispering.

Thus Consuelo, wrapped in her own thoughts, was not as alert as she might have been. It was a startled gasp from Whiskey Jenny that first warned her of danger. But that warning came too late.

Above Rondeen's camp a big-bodied man had spurred out of a brushy thicket, driving his horse straight toward the wagon, studiously managing to keep the wagon between himself and the left wall of the Pass. He came so swiftly that he was alongside the wagon before Consuelo recognized his intent. The only real look she'd ever had at Jube Cazborg had been in distant Rawson, but the savagery in his face was enough to tell her he was no friend. Then he was smothering her in his arms, dragging her from the wagon seat. Kicking and clawing and squirming, she was hauled onto his horse.

"*Señora!*" she screamed at Jenny Rondeen. "Lash the horses! Run fast!"

Rifles began to yammer from the left slope, wild shouts of rage accompanying the spiteful snarl of the guns, but those shots were going wide, for McQuade's guards were handicapped by Consuelo's closeness to Jube Cazborg. And now other riders were pouring out of the thicket to the right, horsemen who came swarming to commandeer the wagon before Jenny could whip up the team and make an escape. Prominent among these riders was black-garbed Caesar Rondeen.

"How do you do, Miss McQuade," he smiled, sweeping his hat away and making a quick bow. "Jube, put her on the ground. Visitors are coming, I see."

Slipping out of his saddle, Cazborg still held the struggling girl. A man was darting from the brush of the left slope, a tall, grizzled Texan who had called Angus McQuade friend for twenty years. "You can't get away with this, Rondeen!" he shouted. "Eleven rifles are covering you from the slope. Angus McQuade's been easy so far. He's only asked you to keep out of the Basin. But if you don't turn that gal loose pronto, there ain't gonna be a man of your outfit left alive."

"So?" Caesar Rondeen murmured soothingly, but hell was aflame in his eye, and the gun that materialized in his hand prodded Consuelo's ribs. "A showdown, eh? And you hold all the aces, *Tejano?* A flick of your finger, and your men burn us down. Chances are, I'd only get in one shot, mister. Just one shot!"

His gun bored deeper into Consuelo's side. "Is that the way you want it?"

The tan fled from the Texan's face, leaving a ghastly ashiness in its place. He swallowed twice before he discovered how to talk again. "You'd shoot her?" he said. "You sneakin' dog, I believe you would."

"He is making the bluff," Consuelo said. "Do not let him get away with it, Ben!"

But Ben wasn't so sure, and his doubt and his fear stood naked in his eyes.

"Patience is its own reward, they say," Rondeen went on easily. "Sooner or later I was bound to find the way to crack through McQuade's armor. You'll get your riflemen out of the brush and have them headed back into the Basin in ten minutes, mister. Otherwise you can burn all the powder you wish. And afterwards you can explain to Angus McQuade why his daughter is dead when a little horse sense on your part would have kept her alive."

Ben was no coward, but he was also no fool. Had the situation been reversed, the gun aimed at his own heart instead of Consuelo's, he might have made a play. As it was, indecisiveness held him silent for a long moment, and his surrender was bitter and wrathful.

"You win — for the time being," he said. "I'm withdrawing the guards. But be mighty careful with that girl, Rondeen. If she's hurt, pulling a mountain down on top of you won't save you from Angus McQuade."

Turning, he walked stiffly away, and within the allotted time he and his guards were ahorse and heading into the Basin. Thus had Caesar Rondeen taken a pat hand, and he smiled thinly, saying, "We'll break camp, boys. I don't think Angus McQuade's deadline means a great deal any more. In fact, I'm going to see him now and deliver an ultimatum. Jube, you and Yampa and Pete take Miss McQuade to the place we had in mind when we first planned this little coup. You might as well take Whiskey Jenny, too. Doc, you come along with me. I've got a special chore for you, once I see McQuade."

He bestowed his smile upon Consuelo. "You're to be our guest, my dear," he said. "Please be assured that you'll be treated with the utmost consideration. You're far too valuable to be harmed in any way."

But Consuelo had wrapped herself in haughty silence, her scornful glance erasing Rondeen's smile. And in silence she watched as Rondeen and Doc Menafee rode away to the north and Rondeen's trail wolves went about breaking up camp. Three or four tents and certain other gear were loaded into Jenny Rondeen's wagon, and Consuelo was forced into the back end of it, along with Whiskey Jenny. Jube Cazborg took the reins, and the two called Yampa and Pete paced the wagon on either side as it headed into the Basin.

Then the miles began to unreel, the sun climbing overhead the while, the wagon jolting and lurching along. From where she sat,

Consuelo had a limited glimpse of sky and trail, and she could only guess that they were veering steadily northward and were well into the Basin. Once Jenny Rondeen leaned over and patted her hand reassuringly, and Consuelo smiled without a great deal of humor.

"I am not worrying," she insisted. "This Rondeen bluff Ben and the guards, but he will not make the bluff on Angus McQuade. Before the sun is set my *padre* will come with many men and many guns to take us away from these *hombres*. Rondeen will not hold us long, *Señora*."

But an hour later when the wagon came to a halt and the prisoners were hauled from it, Consuelo gazed upward, her eyes widening as she saw their ultimate destination. And because she was looking at Satan's own stronghold, a fortress designed by the devil himself, part of the valiant heart went out of her, and she knew that Caesar Rondeen had planned this stroke all too well. Angus McQuade was bested, and no mistake about it.

At that very moment, miles to the south, Mitch Loring was stepping up into a saddle, and, since there was a question in Billy Wing's eyes as he watched the King's kid, Mitch said, "I've got to go look for him, Billy. I don't know how long it's been since Chan rode off with Doc Menafee, but it's been long enough. How much do you think a flag of truce really means to Caesar Rondeen?"

Billy shrugged. "Chan can take care of hisself," he decided. "But I reckon you might as well have a look-see. You've just about wore your heels off, pacing back and forth since he left. But watch yourself, younker. Angus McQuade's got guards somewhere up the pass, remember."

"I'll be careful," Mitch promised, and rode away. But no one challenged him as he headed north, and at last he was abreast of the place where Caesar Rondeen had camped. Gone now were the tents, but the proof that they'd been here was as plain to Mitch as it had been to Chan. His handsome face knotted in puzzlement. Mitch tried to make some sense out of the sign. Then he was loping onward, and still no man tried to block his way.

Had Angus McQuade been bluffing when he'd claimed that sentries were posted in the Pass? And where was Chan? If Doc Menafee had really taken Chan to Caesar Rondeen, then Chan was obviously in the Basin — and so was Rondeen. Yet McQuade had declared that neither Caesar Rondeen nor the Lorings dare cross his deadline.

There were a lot of things that didn't fit into any coherent pattern, Mitch decided, and a nameless dread began to grow upon him, more awesome than the creeping shadows. But still he headed northward, and, thus riding, he saw a knot of horsemen ahead. And because red-bearded McQuade centered the group, Mitch held his horse to a walk and came forward with his hands upraised to signify his desire for a truce.

"I'm Mitch Loring, McQuade, and I'm not here to make trouble," he said. "I'm looking for Chan, mister. He went to see Caesar Rondeen under a white flag. Any idea where I'll find the pair of them?"

"R-rondeen!" Angus McQuade said dully, and it came to Mitch that McQuade had lost all his surety of a few hours before. "Tis in Whisper-ring Town ye'll find R-rondeen, lad. And tis probably the law he's laying down to yer brother, the same as he's laid it down to me and my fr-riends. He's beat us, lad."

"What are you saying?" Mitch demanded. "Talk sense, man."

"He's kidnapped my lassie," McQuade said. "She and the woman who was Slade R-rondeen's wife. He got them between him and my guards, do ye ken, and they dared not fire, because of the lass. He's holding them prisoners in the Basin, and he'll not let them go until me and my friends move out of Whis-

215

per-ring, sur-render the land to his gang of cutthroats."

For a long moment Mitch sat his saddle, stunned and stricken, the full portent of Angus McQuade's disclosure sinking into his consciousness. His first impulse was to head into the Basin on the trail of Consuelo and her kidnappers. Yet if a rescue could be arranged as simply as that, why wasn't Angus McQuade on the trail, instead of sitting here, a beaten giant? And what lay in store for the Lazy-L, now that Rondeen had gained today's heady victory?

"You're — you're letting him get away with this?" Mitch muttered. "Can't you cut sign on Consuelo?"

"The sign is plain, lad. All ye have to do is follow the wagon tracks and ye'll find her. But there's no taking her away from them, Lor-ring. Do ye think I wouldn't be trying if there was a wee chance?"

Whirling his horse about, Mitch galloped back down the Pass, forming plans and discarding them as he rode, but he knew exactly what he was going to do by the time he slithered to a stop before Billy Wing and made a hurried report. Whereupon Billy, his excitement growing as he listened, hitched his gun-belt and said, "This is a job for every hand the Lazy-L's got. Thunder on the Pecos,

216

we'll get that gal and Chan's mother away from Rondeen — or crack a heap of caps trying."

"No." Mitch said. "This is a job for a lone hand. If a bunch of riders could turn the trick, McQuade would be on the trail. Besides, we've got the herd to think about, Billy. The only reason I came back is to tell you to have the boys keep an eye cocked for trouble. Maybe Rondeen *wants* us to leave the longhorns standing while we all ride hell-for-leather into the Basin. But I'm riding alone."

"Chan said you was the boss from here on out," Billy conceded. "And maybe you're right about Rondeen figgering on hitting at the herd. Good luck, son. Ride like hell."

And Mitch did, coming up the Pass again like a man possessed. Once into Whispering Basin, he soon cut sign, seeing spoor to indicate that many men and wagons had headed toward Whispering Town. But he was only interested in the trail of the one lone wagon with its pacing horsemen that had gone on toward the north, and he followed that trail, skirting the east wall of the Basin. When darkness came and there was no moonlight to guide him, he used matches time and again, and always the sign was plain, for there was no regular wagon road this way, and the heavy wheels had made twin creases in the grassy carpet of the Basin.

Then the moon came up, shedding a day-like luminosity on the land, and in the first chalky light Mitch saw Jenny Rondeen's wagon ahead, silent and motionless. Mitch came down out of his saddle then, approaching the wagon stealthily his gun in his hand; but his caution wasn't necessary, for the wagon was empty, and the team that had drawn it was unharnessed and picketed nearby.

Above Mitch, a white cliff glimmered in the moonlight, pale and ethereal, a gaunt upthrust that might have been made by some capricious giant who'd sheared off the hillside at this point, leaving it perpendicular, the cliff facing west with slopes flanking it to the north and south. A series of switchbacks crawled up the slope to the north of the cliff, and a campfire winked far above on the clifftop. And suddenly Mitch knew where Caesar Rondeen had sent his captives, and, with the knowledge, he realized how effectively Angus McQuade's hands had been tied.

Scant chance of a party of men storming that clifftop. To do so they'd have to climb the switchbacks, and the men atop the cliff could pick them off easily enough. Thus, as he sized up the situation, the heart went out of Mitch Loring, just as Consuelo's heart had dropped with the realization of where she was being taken. But stubborn determination tightened Mitch's jaw, and, gun in hand, he started up the switchbacks.

An hour before, he'd been wishing mightily for moonlight to show him the way. Now he prayed that the moon would hide its face and it did, only for a few minutes, sailing into a fleecy cloud bank and out again. But Mitch utilized those minutes to work his way upward, hugging close to such cover as he could find.

Now, panting and heaving, he'd almost finished the ascent, and he had a glimpse of the cliff-top, a shelf some thirty feet wide, the slope rearing on upward behind the shelf, a few tents pitched against the slope, with a fire burning before them, almost on the edge of the cliff. Here on the north edge of the shelf, where the switchbacks ended, there was a cluster of boulders, and Mitch wormed among them, easing forward. But somewhere in that stealthy march he was halted by the pressure of steel against his spine. A man had slid out of the boulders behind him, a man with a gun.

"You pore fool," said Jube Cazborg. "Do you think we ain't been watchin' you since the moment you piled off your hoss down below? No man can reach this cliff-top without us seein' him coming."

Two others came out of the shadows, Pete

and Yampa. Since these were trail wolves who'd joined Rondeen at Dodge, Mitch had never seen them before. Not that it mattered. A growing rage and a black despair gripped him, but neither was effective against a loaded six-gun.

"The last time I was this close to you," Cazborg went on, "the boss was giving me orders to take you out and make a good Injun outa you. That was down in Dodge City, but seein' as that order maybe still holds —"

"Better not burn him down — not right away," Yampa interjected. "The boss seems to have the notion that live prisoners are more valuable than dead ones. Maybe this gent'll be an ace for him, same as the gal and the old woman."

Cazborg shrugged. "Tie him up," he ordered. "Rondeen said to treat the gal and Whiskey Jenny gentle, but we can use our own judgment about this galoot."

Prodded along by Cazborg's gun, Mitch was herded toward the tents. Consuelo's head poked from one of them, her eyes going wide with fear as she saw who'd fallen into Cazborg's hands. Whereupon Mitch grinned ruefully her way and said, "For the gent who comes galloping to the rescue of the fair lady in distress, I shore made a mess of things."

"Shut up," Cazborg ordered, and struck

Mitch across the mouth with the back of his hand. Pete had fetched a lariat and Mitch was quickly trussed, tumbled into a tent. And there in the darkness he reflected upon his fate, and thus bedded with bitterness. He'd come to rescue Rondeen's prisoners, and he'd failed miserably. Worse than that, he'd stumbled right into Cazborg's arms himself. Truly, the game was going Rondeen's way tonight.

But even as hope died within Mitch Loring, it rose again, for he'd been tugging at his bonds, and the rope that held his wrists gave a little. Not much — but now Mitch squirmed and rolled, struggling desperately to loosen the ropes around his wrists.

He was to spend most of the night in that frantic fight. And while he toiled, bathed in perspiration, he laid his plans, knowing that to free himself would only be the first of many obstacles he'd have to surmount if he were to escape.

Consuelo and Jenny Rondeen hadn't been tied. That much Cazborg had admitted, and Consuelo's appearance at the tent flap was proof of it. But the girl and the woman would be closely guarded, which meant that at least one of Rondeen's trio of guards wasn't sleeping this night. Yet if he, Mitch, could get free, he might be able to make a run for it. Perhaps he could take Jenny and Consuelo along with him. If he couldn't rescue both of them, he'd at least try to save Consuelo, for her captivity gave Rondeen the whip-hand, and Whiskey Jenny was a less important pawn who'd probably be released anyway. And if he could get his hands on a gun . . .

Thus he laid his plans, wondering if they were foredoomed to failure even as he made them. The long night dragged its weary way, and the dawn came. And with the first pale flush of morning spreading over Whispering Basin, the last knot gave, and Mitch slipped free of the rope. Time had worked against him, he reflected angrily, for daylight lessened his chances. Coming to his feet, he chaffed his wrists, feeling the sting of re-awakened circulation, and then he eased toward the flap of the tent. It was now or never.

Chapter Nineteen

When Chan Loring came again to Whispering, night had long since fallen and against the ebony backdrop of the all-enveloping gloom, the lights of the settlement were like a sprinkling of stardust, tiny pin points which on other nights had promised food and warmth and shelter to weary wayfarers. But because yonder town had become a citadel of evil by virtue of Caesar Rondeen's presence, the sight of it only stirred a savage fury within Chan.

Across the miles from the Lazy-L herd he'd ridden with a growing rage and a gnawing fear, and from these two had come a desperation that blinded him to everything save the need to find Consuelo and Jenny Rondeen, and Mitch, who'd taken their trail. Thus he swung down from his saddle before the building which housed Caesar Rondeen, and strode fearlessly inside, paying no heed to the hardcases who filled the barroom. Climbing the stairs to Rondeen's office, he found the one-eyed man exactly where he'd left him. And with his back to the door, Chan clipped off brief words.

"Where have you taken her, Rondeen?" he asked.

"You speak of Miss McQuade, I suppose?" Rondeen countered, not one whit perturbed. "Or are you referring to your mother? I recall that you grew quite angry in the Comanche camp when I spoke slightingly of Whiskey Jenny. So it would seem that I dealt myself two aces today, instead of one. Perhaps you'll consider my offer of a few hours ago a little differently now. You didn't seem to believe Whispering was mine when I told you so. I might have offered proof then, but I felt you'd be more impressed if you learned the truth for yourself."

"Never mind that," Chan said. "Where is she, Rondeen? Don't make me force you to talk."

Rondeen shrugged. "It's no secret," he said. "Just follow the east wall of the Basin and you'll come to a place where the slope of a hill has been sheared off to form a cliff that rears upward a good many hundred feet. On top of that cliff there's a shelf, about thirty feet wide, I'd say — room for a comfortable camp. You can reach the cliff-top by climbing a series of switchbacks on the sloping hillside to the north of it. Miss McQuade and your mother are up there, under the watchful eye of Jube Cazborg and others. A natural fortress, that cliff-top. I spotted it the first day I was in Whispering, just before Angus McQuade ordered me out of the Basin."

Lunging through the doorway, Chan was heading for the stairs when Rondeen called him back.

"It's only fair to warn you that Jube has a keg of blasting powder on the cliff-top with him," Rondeen smiled. "Also, a length of fuse. If Angus McQuade gathers his men and attempts to rush the cliff, Jube will merely have to light the fuse and start the keg rolling down the slope. You should have seen old Angus' face when I told him that. Of course in the case of a solitary invader like yourself or the impetuous Mitch, who lately headed into the Basin sniffing wagon tracks like a flea-bitten hound, our Jube won't be so extravagant with his armament. He'll merely pick you off with his six-shooter as you come puffing up the switchbacks. Rather a grim prospect, eh?"

"And you think *that* will stop me?" Chan asked.

"You're a fool, Chan," Rondeen said. "Did you suppose that merely kidnapping Consuelo McQuade would draw old Angus' fangs? He'd be rousing the Basin ranchers for a fight right now if he thought he had any chance to get the girl. But I've got him where the hair's short — and you, too, for that matter. And

225

Mitch will go blundering right into Jube's hands like a fly walking into a spider's web. Now, go and have a look at the set-up. It's the only way you'll be convinced that I hold all the aces."

Turning on his heel, Chan clattered down the stairs, no man in the barroom making a move to stop him, which was in itself a token of the surety of Caesar Rondeen. Into his saddle again, Chan pointed his horse to the north and the east, heading for the hills that rimmed the Basin in that direction, and spurring desperately.

Caesar Rondeen was certain that no man could reach that cliff-top. Caesar Rondeen was so sure of himself that he'd unhesitantly told Chan where the captives were being held. But Chan still clung to his original intention, and his intention was to snatch the captives away from Rondeen. Thus he put the miles behind him, hurrying as fast as he dared in the darkness, thankful when a belated moon edged over the eastern hills and climbed aloft to turn the Basin into a place of shadowy beauty.

And in that chalky light, Chan first saw the cavalcade winding out of the north, a dozen heaped wagons stretched along in single file, men and women and children seated upon them. And in the lead, bowed over his reins, was a red-whiskered giant turned years older in less than the span of a day.

"McQuade," Chan called as he whirled his horse alongside that lead wagon. "Where're you going?"

"Ah, tis King Lor-ring's other cub," McQuade said, peering. "If it's to gloat that ye've come, then gloat ye can. It's wee satisfaction ye'll get out of me, mon."

"You're talking crazy," Chan said. "Why should I gloat because Rondeen's got you where he wants you? I asked you where you're heading."

"Tis until sunr-rise that R-rondeen's given me and my friends to get out of the Basin, lad. If we leave, he'll give me back my lassie. I canna even put up a fight with the gir-rl at stake."

"Look," Chan asked, "is this Basin big enough for you and your friends and the Lazy-L? Don't you see, McQuade? We're together in this thing — both of us against Rondeen's outfit. I'm going after Consuelo now. Maybe one man, alone, will stand a chance of reaching that clifftop. And once she's safe, we can team up against Rondeen. He's got a sizeable pack, and now that he's taken Whispering Town, he'll be mighty hard to budge. But if we should beat him together, we'll share the Basin together. What do you say?"

Angus McQuade lifted his eyes, and there

was a new light of hope in them. "I never meant to hog this land, lad. But when ye fir-rst came, ye filed on all the land. 'Twas drive ye out with yer longhor-rns or be driven out. Do ye ken why I met ye with guns this mor-rning?"

"I filed on the land because that's what King Loring sent me to do," Chan explained. "It was for him to say whether he needed all of it. But the King's dead, and my brother Mitch is boss. He's willing to share the Basin, McQuade. Do we work together?"

Angus McQuade extended his hand. "Tis fighting I like better than r-running," he said. "And a hard fight it will be. I canna refuse, lad."

"Then amble on south," Chan said, taking his hand. "Head to where the Lazy-L herd is bedded and tell Billy Wing about our deal. If I'm not back in twenty-four hours, the two of you can decide what move to make. Be seein' you."

Then Chan was spurring on, a man with renewed hope, flanking the queue of wagons and thundering into the night, putting more miles behind him, until at last he saw the white cliff to the right. At the base of the cliff stood a familiar wagon, the one Jenny Rondeen had ridden from Texas. Cazborg had fetched the captives here in it, likely, Chan reasoned, but had been forced to leave the wagon below, since not even a saddler could climb the switchbacks on the north slope to the clifftops. And here Chan slid from his horse, studying the situation, then moving forward on foot.

Ignoring the switchbacks, he chose to climb the slope on the southern side of the cliff, finding the going hard, for in places the rise was almost straight up, and brush and timber made troublesome barriers. Sweating and straining, he toiled on upward, digging his heels into the turf and reaching for hand-holds wherever he could find them. But it was slow, arduous work, and it was long past midnight before he could gaze to his left and see the shelf-like clifftop.

In the open stretch before the tents, a campfire winked, almost on the cliff's edge, shapeless figures huddling around it. By careful maneuvering, Chan might have worked over to the shelf at this point, but the chances were great that Rondeen's men would hear him coming. Instead, Chan climbed on upward, another two hours finding him out of the timber and on a shale-mottled slope, where he edged northward until at last he was looking down upon the enemy camp and the Basin below it.

Dawn would soon be breaking, he realized.

He'd seen no sign of Mitch, though far beneath him, in the dark bowl of the Basin, he thought he saw a horse moving. Whether it was Mitch's or his own, he couldn't tell. Mitch must be somewhere close, he guessed. And then, when the sun limned the eastern hills with the first pale flush of dawn, he discovered Mitch.

First Chan began to perceive movement on the shelf below him, figures scurrying about, and as he watched, his eyes strained, they began to take shape, and suddenly he realized he was looking upon drama, an angry frustration filling him because he was too far away to take part in it.

For that was Mitch down there, bobbing out of a tent and rushing toward another one. And when Mitch reappeared, he had Consuelo by the hand, and the two of them were running toward the north, sprinting for those switchbacks that led down into the Basin. So Mitch had been here all the time, then. Probably Mitch had blundered into Cazborg's grasp, Chan guessed. Probably he'd been trussed and tossed into a tent. But Mitch had managed to get free, and now he was making a break for it.

A hoarse shout floated up to Chan. Men came converging from all points of the clifftop, the huge bulk of Jube Cazborg darting from the rim, others bobbing from the region of the tents. A gun barked, the sound thin and waspish, and Mitch stumbled, went to one knee, came erect again, apparently uninjured, and continued running, dragging Consuelo after him.

The shelf stretched for no more than a hundred and fifty feet. Chan found himself staring breathlessly, watching that race below, and his heart called out, *"Hurry, Mitch!"* though his lips remained locked. His gun was poised in his hand, but the time to shoot was lost.

For, with bullets nipping his heels, Mitch had come to a stop and was standing with hands upraised, Cazborg and the others running toward him. And with Mitch's shoulders slumping in surrender, Consuelo suddenly threw her arms about him, kissing him fervently. The two of them were entwined together when Cazborg and his men laid hands on them, dragging the pair back to the tents.

All this Chan saw, and the sight left him stricken, the evidence of Consuelo's love for Mitch a blow that was softened only because the re-capture of the two of them was a greater blow. Thus he hunkered on the slope, numb and motionless, watching while Cazborg's men trussed Mitch securely and thrust him into a tent.

And still Chan watched, wondering if he

might inch down the slope, come onto the camp from above, yet remain undetected until he was within striking distance. He saw Jenny Rondeen now, squatting before a tent slump-shouldered and motionless, and he saw a powder keg between two other tents. Then Rondeen's three men were gathered in a knot that soon untangled itself, Jube Cazborg standing alone while the others filed toward the switchbacks and began a descent.

At first their departure made no sense to Chan, and then he understood the reason for it. Strategic as this clifftop was, its one disadvantage was that it was cut off from supplies. A man with a rifle might hold it against an invading horde, but only so long as his food and water and ammunition lasted. Obviously those two were going to Whispering for supplies, and probably to report to Rondeen as well. Jube Cazborg would do the guarding alone until they returned.

Here was opportunity, the sight of it sucking in Chan's breath. Very cautiously he began to ease down the slope, finding that descending was more ticklish than climbing had been. He was halfway to the shelf when the pair who'd left emerged from a clump of trees far below and rode off. No chance now of their hearing any commotion on the cliff-top. But in the midst of that comforting thought, disaster struck Chan. Inching downward another foot or so, he suddenly found himself unable to stop. The earth had come to life and he was caught in a small landslide of his own making, hurtling downward upon the camp.

His wild fear in that awful moment was that the momentum of the slide would carry him across the width of the shelf and over the cliff to his doom. Shooting over the edge of a cutback, he cleared the top of the low tents, hitting the shelf and rolling to a stop at the feet of Jube Cazborg. Staring with startled eyes, Cazborg's swarthy face twisted as he recognized who'd made such a spectacular entry. Instantly, Chan wrapped his arms around the man's legs, bringing him down.

Then they were locked together, twisting and turning and rolling dangerously near the rim of the cliff. It was a fight on eternity's edge, and Consuelo, who hadn't been tied, burst from her tent shrilling, "Chan! Kill him! Kill him, Chan!" Jenny Rondeen was on her feet, her eyes wide, watching the struggle.

There was a lot of strength in Cazborg's body, and he wrenched free, coming erect and lunging backward a step or two. At once Chan was on his feet and after the man, but in that moment his chances for victory dissolved before the certainty of defeat. For Jube Cazborg had wrenched his gun free and was holding it, the hammer eared back.

"Hoist 'em." he panted. "Hoist 'em, damn you." And Chan slowly obeyed, knowing the game was up, and tasting the bitter gall of hopelessness.

Whereupon Consuelo calmly stepped over to the powder keg, just as calmly struck a match and touched it to the end of the fuse.

Chan saw her do it. And because the act seemed so utterly mad, so utterly useless, he comprehended her intention not at all. Cazborg saw it too, and bellowed wildly, "Put that out," fear draining some of the darkness from his face. "Are you loco, you damn hell-cat? Put that fuse out, or I'll shoot you."

"No," Consuelo said firmly. "First you drop the gun. Or go ahead and shoot, *chivo*. But the fuse it will still burn, and the *polvora* it will go boom!"

Putting her back to the wild-eyed gunman, she stepped into Mitch's tent, only to bob into view a moment later, Mitch following after her, chaffing his wrists.

Cazborg had made no move to stop her. "For gawd's sake put that fuse out," he blubbered. "You, Mitch Loring, show some sense! Don't you savvy? We'll *all* be blasted to hell if the fire hits that powder."

It was a moment when the sun stood still in the heavens, a grim tableau that Chan would

234

remember always: Jube Cazborg standing there, his gun wavering, the man unable to move to pluck the fuse from the keg, since one Loring or the other might find the chance to jump him if he made the try — Chan trying to keep his eyes off the shortening fuse, watching Cazborg for the first sign that the gunhawk might be off guard — Mitch staring wide-eyed, just comprehending the situation — Jenny Rondeen with one hand faltering to her throat, her face gray. And Consuelo, the calmest of them all, obviously enjoying this moment.

"Hurry!" Cazborg cried, a thin rind of sweat forming on his upper lip. "Hurry, or we'll all be dead."

"First, throw down the gun," Consuelo insisted stubbornly.

It was nerve against nerve, a game of bluff with death as the dealer, a grinning spectre who'd rake in the stakes no matter who won. It was more than flesh and blood could hear, and within Chan there was a wild urge to shout, to beg Consuelo to jerk that sputtering fuse. With it inching toward the powder, somebody had to crack. And Jube Cazborg did.

"You win," he sobbed, and hurled his gun away, taking two instinctive steps backward at the same time, putting that much more distance between himself and the powder keg.

Then everything happened at once. Cazborg, in taking those two steps, had backed away from one kind of peril and into another, for he'd forgotten how close he stood to the cliff's edge. Just for an instant he was poised on the rim, his arms flailing, fighting to regain his balance. Chan lunged toward him, but Chan moved too late. For with a wild cry of despair, Jube Cazborg disappeared, his scream of terror trailing after him. Leaning over, Chan had one horrible glimpse of a twisting thing of arms and legs hurtling downward.

Now Consuelo was running, grasping Jenny Rondeen by the elbow and dragging her along, heading as fast as feet could carry her toward a cluster of boulders near the switchbacks. And Chan understood. That fuse was far too short to risk an attempt to pluck it. Yet Mitch was moving toward the keg, patently intending to make such a try.

"No Mitch. Run for it." Chan screamed and bounded to his foster-brother, seizing him and dragging him away.

Only then did Mitch seem to realize how near to death they stood, and together the two Lorings turned and sprinted after Consuelo and Whiskey Jenny. But somewhere in the midst of that race the powder let go, a wall of wind hitting the two Texans, hurling them to the rocky floor of the shelf as thunder dinned.

They came to their feet with their clothes half-torn from them, their faces smoke-be-grimed and bloody. Each looked like a man out of hell at that moment, and Chan, seeing the horror in Mitch's eyes, wondered if they mirrored his own. And then he was laughing hysterically, for he realized that no more harm had come to Mitch than had befallen himself.

It was Jenny Rondeen who failed to understand that neither of them had been seriously hurt. And it was Jenny Rondeen who amazed Chan. She came running back toward them, her face twisted with anguish, and thus, for the first time since he'd known her, she was all human — a mother.

"But hers is the heart of a mother, Chan," Consuelo had once said. "And there will come a day when it will call aloud and you will hear it." And now Jenny Rondeen was seeing the flesh of her flesh bloody and bruised, and she was coming to her son with arms outstretched. And because the heart of her had finally spoken, all of Chan Loring's life was forever altered . . .

Chapter Twenty

He came out of Whispering Pass in the afternoon of that same day, putting his back to the grazing herd of Lazy-L longhorns, and facing away from his gathered friends, a man headed for a long-awaited rendezvous with destiny.

Less than an hour before, he'd driven Jenny Rondeen's wagon down out of the Basin, coming unchallenged from the cliff to those who waited in the Pass, and there he'd witnessed the reunion of Consuelo and her father, and seen the Basin ranchers and the Lazy-L seal a pact of friendship. There'd been great rejoicing among all of them, the happiness of it tempered only by the thought that a fight against odds lay ahead. And in the midst of it all, Chan had called Billy Wing aside and given him certain instructions, then stolen quietly away. And now Chan Loring rode back toward town alone.

Thus he came to Whispering Town for the third time, riding up the straggly street and finding it singularly deserted in the hazy heat of this languid autumn afternoon. But the long line of wagons was still here, and there were horses before Caesar Rondeen's headquarters, and the sign of the Spur Wheel had been hoisted above the door since Chan had been here last. The tinny piano rattled away, hammering about the whir of a roulette wheel, and it was Chan's thought that only the surroundings had changed and this was as Texas had been.

When he came through the door, the piano player saw him first and leaned upon a note too long, that old discordant signal swinging Doc Menafee away from the bar, just as it had fetched Jube Cazborg around another time. But Jube Cazborg was dead now, a heap of stones piled over him at the base of a distant cliff, and Doc Menafee's wolfish grin was a little forced. With that same old hushed expectancy falling upon the few men within the room, Chan crossed in the throbbing stillness and mounted to Rondeen's office above.

He entered quietly, and he closed the door behind him, standing with his back to it and facing Caesar Rondeen across the man's desk. If faint surprise touched Rondeen's bony features, the sign of it was only there for an instant, his unctuous smile spreading to erase it.

"Ah, Chan," Rondeen sighed. "Congratulations are in order, it seems. Two of my boys came into town this morning to report that all was well atop the rock. They'd managed to capture young Mitch last evening, and they'd hog-tied him. Mitch wriggled loose and made a dash for freedom, so the report went, but they'd fetched him back. But when my boys came quirting into town a few hours later, they were singing a different tune. Someone had heaved our blood-thirsty Jube over the rim, meanwhile, and walked off with the prisoners. Naturally they suspected that Mitch had gotten free again. But I guessed differently. That, said I, was the work of a Rondeen. Was I right, Chan?"

"Partly," Chan admitted. "Consuelo and Jenny are back in the Pass, Rondeen. McQuade's outfit and the Lazy-L have joined forces. I reckon you know what that means. They'll raid Whispering before the day is through."

At a moment when Caesar Rondeen should have been amazed, he appeared to be only perplexed. "A word of warning from you, Chan?" he mused. "Am I to infer that at the final showdown your blood is beginning to tell? Ah, but that grim look betrays you. It isn't our kinship that fetched you here."

"I've come," said Chan, "to tell you a story."

"A story?"

"It has to do with Whiskey Jenny," Chan

amplified. "Rondeen, did you ever wonder what went through her mind on that day when she lay in Doc Turlock's house in Rawson, a baby in her arms, and heard that Slade had gone down beneath King Loring's gun? It was a bad hour for her, I know. In the next room was King Loring's wife, also with her first-born. Jenny told me herself that if the King's wife hadn't been dead from childbirth, Jenny would have crawled to her and choked the life out of her. As it was, Jenny was pretty nearly crazy that day.

"In the next room was King Loring's kid — the baby who'd grow up on the fat of the land and inherit the mighty Lazy-L when the King passed on. In Jenny's arms was her own child, half-an-orphan, a kid who'd never have anything but kicks and abuse all his days. It was a pretty grim future the son of Slade Rondeen faced — especially when you compared it to the lot of King Loring's kid. So maybe you can guess what Whiskey Jenny, knowing these things, did."

"I believe I can," said Caesar Rondeen, and his voice had sunk to a whisper.

"She switched babies, of course, crawling into the other room and putting her own child beside the King's wife, and taking the other baby back with her. Don't you see, Rondeen? She had a double purpose in mind. First, she was getting revenge on King Loring. And, at the same time, she was insuring the right kind of raising for her own kid."

"It makes sense." Caesar Rondeen mused. "You never looked like the Rondeens, Chan, but, for that matter, neither does Mitch. You're both a pair of throw-backs, I guess. That's why the King never suspected the truth, nor I. So Whiskey Jenny only told me half the truth when I made her tell me what had become of Slade's kid. She said she'd turned the baby over to King Loring, but she never gave a hint that she'd switched babies the day the two of you were born."

"It must have been quite a surprise to Jenny when the King looked her up in Amarillo and offered to take me to raise," Chan went on. "That was something she shore hadn't counted on, and at first she wouldn't let him have me. But she finally gave me to the King because she'd figgered out that that didn't change anything. After all, it was still Mitch who was *supposed* to be the King's kid — and it was Mitch who'd be the King's heir. So what difference did it make what become of me?"

"Whiskey Jenny had more brains than I suspected," Rondeen remarked, a man visibly impressed. "You see, I never had any use for her, and I hated Slade for marrying her. But it appears she had more sense than anyone ever gave her credit for having."

"She played her game almost to the finish," Chan continued. "That night in Rawson when you told me what you thought was the truth, I went to see her. I had to decide whether I'd take the Lazy-L herd to Montana, and she urged me to do it. That surprised me some, seeing as she hated King Loring. But, like always, she was watching out for Mitch, her son. *I* was to sweat to get the herd to Whispering, but it would still be Mitch's herd. In the Nations, when I clouted Mitch off his horse, I saw the look on her face and should have guessed that Mitch meant something to her. But I thought she was only showing a woman's squeamishness at the sight of violence. It wasn't until today that the truth came out."

"It was she who told you, of course," Rondeen guessed. "But why?"

"That powder keg went off on the clifftop," Chan explained. "Never mind how. The explosion messed up me and Mitch some, though we weren't really hurt. But we looked bad, I reckon, and the sight was too much for Jenny. You savvy? She thought Mitch was dying, *and she ran to Mitch.* When she started babbling about her baby, her arms around Mitch, the whole truth came out. On top of that, Jenny's conscience had been working. I'd saved her life the day of the prairie fire, and that hit her hard, owing her life to a Loring. And the King had treated her mighty decent, and so did I — seeing as I thought she was my mother. But it's Mitch who's Slade Rondeen's son."

Caesar Rondeen passed a hand through his sweep of salt-and-pepper hair, most of the surety gone out of him. But that was only for a moment, his composure quickly returning.

"So?" he said. "And now the cards are faced, and the truth is known. But that naturally leads to one last question. What fetched you here, Chan?"

"Something that started over twenty years ago, I reckon," Chan said flatly. "Something that has to be finished today. You see, the King made me promise that I'd never match gunsmoke with you. But that was because he thought I was your kin, and he knew I'd regret gunning you if I ever learned the truth. But because I'm a Loring and you're a Rondeen, that promise I made doesn't hold any more, mister."

"Meaning?"

"Two things fetched me here," Chan said. "One is the hope that if I down you, your wolves will give up the fight, and no McQuade or Lazy-L blood will have to be spilled. Naturally, it hit Mitch hard when he found he was a Rondeen, just as it hit me that night in Rawson. But the Lazy-L will ride against Whispering just the same. The other reason I'm here is because you're the man who killed King Loring, and I couldn't take the chance that somebody else might catch you in their sights. He was my father, Rondeen. I'm a Loring. Now are you ready to start your smoke?"

Whereupon Caesar Rondeen laughed, his head tipped back, and the bony length of him shaking with merriment.

"You're still a fool, Chan," he said. "Don't you suppose that the minute I learned that Consuelo had escaped I knew what would follow? And I know just how old Angus and those wild Texans of yours will wage war. They'll come loping into Whispering like a troop of cavalry charging an Indian camp. Did you notice that the street is empty? There's a rifleman posted on every roof-top and porch, others hidden in the wagons. They could have shot you out of your saddle today if I'd wished it. You'll never leave Whispering alive, Chan. And when your friends come riding, they'll ride straight into a carefully planned trap."

"Not if I warn them first," Chan said. "I'll take my chances on getting out of here. Will you make your play, Rondeen?"

But Caesar Rondeen's fingers strayed to the

metal box on the top of his desk, the box Chan and Mitch had both wanted so desperately.

"I told you once that as a gambler I found it expedient to have an extra ace or two handy," Rondeen said. "Maybe I'm down to my last one. You know what this box contains, I suppose. Then take it —."

If his talk had served no other purpose, it had at least lulled Chan into a moment of unwariness. Thus he was unprepared as Rondeen suddenly hurled the metal box at his face. Instinctively Chan dodged, the box whizzing past his head to strike the wall and clatter into a corner. But that one unguarded moment was all Caesar Rondeen needed. His hands slipped behind his desk, moving like striking snakes, and when they flashed into sight again they clutched a sawed-off shotgun aimed at Chan's breast.

"So it's a showdown you want." Rondeen said. "Steady there — this scattergun can tear a hole in you as big as your head! You came to tell me you're a Loring, eh? And you want the Loring-Rondeen feud finished forever. Have you stopped to think that now that I know the truth it changes my attitude toward you, too? Here's where I collect final payment for the eye King Loring took from me. Now we'll see how the last of the Lorings dies."

Chapter Twenty-one

This, then, was Caesar Rondeen's last ace, this shotgun he held pointed at Chan. And staring into the black bore of it, Chan knew he was staring at death just as surely as though the shotgun had already spoken. In a man's last moment, he was supposed to think of many things, his life parading before him, but Chan indulged in no such reverie, his only thought being the bitter one that at showdown he'd failed — and failed completely.

What did it matter that he'd come across the miles, bringing the longhorn herd of the Lazy-L all the way to Montana in spite of every obstacle that had loomed? What did it matter that he'd instructed Billy Wing to lead the combined force of the Basin ranchers and the Lazy-L crew against Whispering if he, Chan, were not back at a given time? In the end, the victory was bound to belong to Caesar Rondeen, for Chan Loring would be dead, and his friends would ride unwarned into a trap.

Thus the last hand was going to Rondeen, and the last hand would rake in the stakes. And Caesar Rondeen realized all these things, for he was savoring this moment as a man savors old wine, sipping it slowly and dwelling upon the taste of it. Yet he was a different Caesar Rondeen than Chan had ever known, this man who glared at him over the shotgun's barrel. Gone were the affected mannerisms, the pretense of scholarliness, and he stood revealed for what he was. The stark savagery of him paling into insignificance the brutishness that had been Jube Cazborg's.

"Well," Chan said. "What are you waiting for?" He found nothing familiar about his own voice.

"I'm waiting to see you squirm — or go for your gun if you dare," Rondeen said. "I'm waiting for your nerve to crack so you'll beg for mercy you'll never get from me. I'm waiting to see a Loring on his knees before a Rondeen."

"You'll wait a mighty long time," Chan said.

The shotgun never wavered, and still Chan stared into the barrel of it, the weapon holding his eyes in the same way that an open flame exerts a hypnotic influence.

This couldn't be him, Chan Loring, standing here, he concluded. The scene was too unreal — too much like a wild dream that would eventually bring him sitting bolt upright in his blankets, bathed in perspiration. In a way, it was akin to that moment atop the cliff when a fuse had slowly crawled toward a powder keg and doom. But the difference was that either Consuelo or Jube Cazborg had had to break under that strain, and there'd been a chance for reprieve. There could only be one ending to this episode.

"You're beginning to sweat," Rondeen observed, his face hard and expressionless. "You're straining your ears for hoof-beats, hoping your friends will come. Listen well, Loring. For when they come I'll be needed elsewhere — and I'll finish my business here first."

An eternity crawled by, though the span of it could actually be encompassed in the space of a few clock ticks. By a force of will, Chan dragged his eyes away from the shotgun, seeing in this room many things he'd never noticed before — small things, unimportant things. Yonder, for instance, the chinking had fallen from between two logs, leaving a patch of light in its place, light that was slowly graying as night came on. And —

The door was creaking gently, though Chan had been aware of no sound on the stairs. Caesar Rondeen's expression changed slightly. For less than the space of a heartbeat his eyes flicked toward the doorway. That was all Chan needed. Hurling himself forward, he dodged sideways at the same time, lurching at

Rondeen's blind side, and grasping at the shotgun's barrel as he dived under it.

The *br-r-oo-mpf* of the gun was like a cannon's voice in the confines of the room. And as Chan lunged backwards, wrenching the shotgun from Rondeen's grasp and heaving it aside, he had a brief glimpse of Doc Menafee. It was Menafee who'd opened the door, only to be thrust backward as he stood framed in the doorway, for the full charge of buckshot had caught the gunman in the breast, mutilating him.

Caesar Rondeen was dipping a hand under the tails of his black alpaca coat, dragging a six-shooter into sight, blazing away at Chan. Falling toward the floor, Chan jerked his own gun at the same time, firing blindly and seeing Rondeen take two hesitant steps forward, then sprawl across his desk. So died Caesar Rondeen, who had looked upon Whispering Basin and lusted for it, and so and old debt was paid, an old account closed forever.

And then, with the echoes fading away, two sounds came to Chan out of the smoky silence. One was a commotion in the barroom below, proof that its occupants had been aroused by the gunfire. The other was the muted drumming of hoofs, thundering token that Billy Wing was on the way.

Taking time only to scoop the metal box

from the floor, Chan tucked it inside his shirt and hit the stairs running. Below him three men were clustered, Chan's first shot blowing that huddled knot apart and sending two of them scurrying to corners of the room. The third man stood gazing at the gun he'd aimed at Chan, then slowly crumpled and fell on his face, the gun exploding harmlessly.

But the other two were firing, the piano player was diving behind his instrument with a wild squawk of fear, and into that crossfire Chan plunged, goaded to desperation by the thought that this pair stood between him and the warning he might give Billy Wing, the warning that would save the Lazy-L and its allies from Rondeen's hidden riflemen.

He felt the hot breath of a bullet past his cheek, and he peered through his own powder smoke, trying to locate the two. One had tipped over a gaming table and taken shelter behind it, and Chan managed to catch him in his sights, sending the fellow threshing across the floor. But the other was somewhere in the thronging shadows at this lamp-lighting hour, his lead laying a fiery sword along Chan's ribs, half-wheeling him about. Chan went down on one knee, saving his own life by the action, for a bullet droned overhead. Then Chan snapped a shot at a moving shadow, and saw the last man fling up his arms and die.

But there'd be others out on the street, twenty or more of them, hidden on porch-tops and inside Rondeen's wagons, and with the gun echoes dying away again, Chan's stricken thought was that already he was too late to stop the Lazy-L. The thunder of hoofs had risen to a reverberating crescendo. And as he burst from the Spur Wheel, it came to Chan that something was almighty wrong. A hundred times as many hoofs were beating as should have heralded the coming of the Lazy-L.

In the street, he became acutely aware that a bullet might cut him down before he took three steps. Rondeen's riflemen had stayed at their posts, ignoring the gunfire in the saloon, satisfied, probably, that those who were involved could take care of themselves. But those same riflemen might recognize him and guess his intent and stop him with a bullet. Such was Chan's thought, but it wasn't riflefire that drove him hastily back into the saloon. For Chan had scurried before the sight of something beyond his wildest hopes.

Down upon Whispering Town came the full force of the Lazy-L, and with the Texans were Angus McQuade and his fighting friends. These were the men who might have been mowed down by a withering blast from hidden rifles. But there was no chance of that now. For ahead of the attackers, thundering along in a wild stampede aimed at the straggly street, came the longhorn herd, two thousand charging juggernauts urged on by popping rope-ends and hoarse shouts!

It was a sight that sent a great exultation surging through Chan. Across the weary miles he'd dreaded a stampede, that constant menace to a trail drive, and by dint of his skill he'd managed to prevent such a thing, save on the occasion when the longhorns had bolted to the Canadian after the dry drive. But now the herd was in full stampede, two thousand longhorns gone loco, and Chan blessed the wisdom of Billy Wing who'd found a means to take the town against any odds.

Bellowing wildly, the herd was pouring into the town, lunging down the street, filling it from wall to wall, the leaders pressed forward by the weight of those behind, timbers splintering as they crashed into the supports of wooden awnings. From the doorway of the Spur Wheel, Chan glimpsed part of the chaos wrought by the longhorns, heard the futile roar of rifles.

Rondeen's wolves were making a stand, and some of the longhorn leaders were buckling at the knees, going down. But it was like trying to stop a raging torrent by building a dam out of dewdrops. Full into the line of wagons the herd crashed, canvas billowing as the wagons were overturned, men screaming in terror as they tossed their rifles aside and tried to dash to safety.

Most of the herd had passed the Spur Wheel, and in the vanguard came the whooping riders. Chan sprinted into the street then, catching a glimpse of a Rondeen rifleman plunging downward as a porch collapsed, seeing the man swallowed beneath that sea of bobbing, bony backs.

Some of Rondeen's men had managed to get into saddles and were bee-lining between buildings, scattering for the safety that lay beyond the town. The Lazy-L and the Basin ranchers were instantly after them, Billy Wing streaking past Chan with a wild shout, waving one hand at Chan, firing with the other. Hard on the old man's heels came Angus McQuade, the shrill war cry of his clan bursting from the giant's lips. And Chan, catching up a rearing, riderless horse, was into the fray.

As a fight, it was something of a shambles, for the longhorns had already depleted the ranks of Rondeen's men, and there was little left to do. Dead steers littered the street, some dropped by Rondeen rifles, some killed when they'd crashed into buildings and wagons as that relentless tide had swept forward. Over the town dust billowed, churned by eight thousand hooves, the pall still blending with the twilight, though the herd was beyond the town and scattered over the Basin's floor. But behind them they'd left chaos and destruction and other dead besides their own — shapeless things that had once been men — killers who would kill no more. And in this manner, victory, costly but complete and lasting, came to the men who'd charged out of Whispering Pass this day.

Yonder, Billy Wing was bellowing, "Let the rest of 'em go, boys. Git busy and round up the herd. You're cowpokes again, you rannyhans."

And Angus McQuade, "Ye spoiled all the fun with yer longhor-rns. Tis a fight we wanted, and I dinna ken how ye can fight when there's not a mon left standing. Have ye seen R-rondeen, lads? Tis a lot he's got to answer for, and tis me he'll answer to, unless hell has already claimed its own."

And yonder Mitch Loring came riding, and with him was Consuelo; for who was the man who could keep the daughter of Angus McQuade out of the fight? They rode close together, laughing and talking, and something in that sight cemented a decision for Chan that had begun to shape itself high above the clifftops that very morning when he'd seen Consuelo in Mitch's arms.

Yet, with his decision made, he hesitated, for to do as he planned meant a parting with all the Lazy-L without so much as a word of good-bye. Streaking across the grassland were men who'd shared a dozen dangers with him — Pete Still, Ollie Archer, Holy Joe Hawkins, Billy Wing, Stew Bidwell, and all the others. The memory of the miles they'd crossed together brought a lump to Chan's throat.

Yet the very kinship that had been born of the thundering trail had made a bond between them that would always endure. What did it matter whether he said good-bye with the usual attendant ceremony, when actually there could never be a good-bye between him and the memory of them? Wherever his lonely trail took him, he would still belong to the Lazy-L.

So thinking, he made his choice, lifting his horse to a gallop, and merging with the twilight. And thus he faded from sight and was gone.

Chapter Twenty-two

He'd slept where tiredness had overtaken him, somewhere in the south end of Whispering Pass, for, though he'd wanted to put many miles behind him between sundown and sunrise, he'd had no sleep the night before, and nature had made its demands. He'd bandaged himself with strips torn from his undershirt, finding the wound along his ribs no more than a scratch. And now, with the dawn breaking above the eastern hills, he had one last thing to do before he hurried on.

The metal box that had belonged to Caesar Rondeen lay at his hand when he awoke. After he'd pulled on his boots and saddled his cayuse, he tried to force the box open with a rock, and, failing in that, he shot the lock away. Inside lay a couple of sheets of paper, carefully folded.

"Caesar Rondeen owns a little black metal box," the King had said. "Get it, Chan. And — destroy what's inside it without looking at them papers."

He laid the papers upon the ground and touched a match to a corner of them, and the papers had crumbled away to nothing when he heard the creak of gear and lifted his eyes to see Mitch and Consuelo loping up. He knew then that he'd tarried here too long. From their saddles the pair looked at him wordlessly, Mitch's eyes widening as they flicked to the empty metal box and then to the ashes of the papers it had contained.

"So you *did* have it," Mitch said. "I searched all of Whispering last night for that box, and then I figgered you'd taken it away."

"It's gone now, whatever it was," Chan said and was careful to avoid Consuelo's solemn eyes. "The King asked me to destroy those papers without looking at them. I've finished the chores."

"Then the King knew." Mitch said. "And you've got a right to know too, Chan."

"It doesn't matter," Chan said.

"But it does," Mitch insisted. "You see, Chan, it was a club Caesar Rondeen held over me and over the King, too, looks like. You just burned my signed confession that I was involved in a murder."

"A murder!"

"You know that I hung around with Rondeen a lot," Mitch went on. "Like I told him that day you were along in Rawson, I thought the Loring-Rondeen feud was something that existed mostly in the King's mind,

258

and I thought it was smart to buck the King's wishes by being friendly to Rondeen. I'd taken quite a few *pasears* up into the north with Caesar Rondeen — and I took one too many."

"Into the Nations?" Chan guessed, for a pattern was beginning to shape itself, tearing the veil from the face of mystery.

Mitch nodded. "Like I said in Dodge, Rondeen was the head of an outfit of trail wolves, those same boys we scattered last night. Rondeen kept those boys stretched all the way from Doan's Crossing to Ogallala, and nothing happened along the trail that they didn't know about."

"Yes," Chan agreed. "Rondeen knew every move I'd made when I came north the first time."

"And he knew when old Hank Thompson came down from Ogallala with a satchel full of money he'd gotten from selling a herd that had belonged to him and his neighbors."

"Hank Thompson. The man whose grave we found in the wasteland!" Chan cried. "Was that how come you knew the lay of that land, and didn't want to make the dry drive?"

Again Mitch nodded. "Rondeen had asked me to take a trip with him and Cazborg and Menafee. That was while you were up here in Montana, Chan. I didn't know what was behind Rondeen's notion, but he bee-lined straight for Thompson's camp once we'd cut sign on the old man. Now I can savvy that Rondeen's spies had passed the word along that Thompson had left Ogallala with money. But honest to God, Chan, I didn't tumble until Cazborg put a slug into Thompson, and Rondeen grabbed the money satchel. It was me who buried Thompson and put that marker over him. Rondeen was against the idea of leaving any sign, but I bucked him plenty."

"And those papers in the box admitted you'd had a hand in that deal?"

"Yes," Mitch said. "I'd been gambling heavily in the Spur Wheel, and I owed Rondeen plenty. He threatened to take my I.O.U.'s to the King, and I begged him for time to pay off. He agreed to wait if I'd sign a paper admitting that I'd been mixed up in the Thompson killing, though you can damn well bet the paper didn't mention Rondeen himself. It would be his security, he said, that I wouldn't welsh. And like the drunken fool I was, I signed."

"The night the King died, he told me Rondeen had showed him the box," Chad said. "Likely Rondeen taunted him, telling him what was in the box. That's why the King wanted me to get those papers and destroy them sight unseen."

"We were brothers in his eyes," Mitch said. "He'd have wanted the same if your name had been on the bottom of those papers. And now you've made me a free man, Chan."

"You're not the first kid who blundered into the wrong turn of the trail, Mitch," Chan said. "If you'd really had a hand in Thompson's death, it might be different. As it is, let's pretend that what's been said here is ashes too."

Whereupon Mitch nodded humbly. "You'll do to take along, Chan," he said. "If I'd had half the eye the King had, I'd have seen that from the first. I'm beginning to understand why the King wrote his will as he did."

"Meaning?"

"Here's the will." Mitch fumbled in his chap's pocket and extended a folded sheet of paper. "Billy Wing showed it to me last night. There'd been so much excitement since we hit Whispering that he'd plumb forgot he was packing it."

Very slowly Chan unfolded the sheet of legal foolscap, skimming over the preamble and reading on, seeing the heart and soul of King Loring beneath the legal phraseology of the lawyer, Ezra Pettigrew.

" 'Since I have two sons,' " he read, " 'it behooves me to make provisions for both of them. Therefore my holdings, the Lazy-L, shall be their joint property. But since it has

261

been my observation that no ranch is big enough to have two masters, one must be in charge, the other second to him. And since I have endeavored never to discriminate between my sons, I hereby decree that judgment shall be reserved until the ranch is reestablished in Montana. My old friend William Wing, who is provided for elsewhere in this document, shall be the judge, but actually the trail shall make the decision. Therefore, upon reaching Montana, the said William Wing shall name whichever of my sons has best proved himself on the trail, and that son shall be boss of the Lazy-L, the other to share ownership but to give his unreserved obedience and loyalty to the boss . . .' "

"You see," Mitch said softly. "Even if Jenny hadn't spoken on top of the rock, it would still be you who'd be the boss of the Lazy-L, Chan. Billy doesn't have to tell me that. My bonehead play the day the Comanches came would have disqualified me, alone. It took a just man to write the King's kind of will. I'll always be proud to remember him as my father, even though he wasn't. I'd like to think that I've already proved that I'm Caesar Rondeen's kin by blood only. He was a skunk who had a killing coming to him, and I'll never hold it against you for whatever happened between you and him yesterday, Chan. The Loring-Rondeen feud is really finished. For myself I'm only asking what you asked in Whispering Pass, Chan — a place for Jenny, my mother."

"You'll have that — and more, Mitch," Chan said and wondered how lame his next words would sound. "I'm leaving the Lazy-L to you, boy. I guess Texas is a place I just can't get out of my blood. I'm going back there, Mitch."

But Mitch wasn't fooled for a minute. "Me and Consuelo wondered why you slipped away last night," he said. "We think we figgered out the answer. You saw her kiss me yesterday morning?"

"I couldn't help but see," Chan admitted.

Mitch glanced at the still-faced girl, some message passing wordlessly between them. "So you know that we're in love with each other, Consuelo and I," he said. "It would be too much for you to stay in Whispering and see us building a life together. That's it, eh, Chan? And yet I can't blame you. I reckon it would be the same with me if it was the other way around."

"Maybe I'm a coward, running," Chan said. "I'm glad you understand, Mitch."

"I know," Mitch said regretfully. "And I'm sorry, Chan. Will you shake before you leave?"

263

Wordlessly, Chan took the proferred hand and turned to find Consuelo with her hand extended also. "Goodbye, Chan," she said, more solemn than ever. "The first *niño* we shall name after you. And some day you will ride back and see him. *Si?*"

"Yes," he agreed, but he knew that he was lying, and he quickly turned his back to them, stepping up into his saddle and touching spurs to his cayuse. He didn't look back as he rode away, for behind him was everything he'd ever wanted, and a last look would be less than nothing to take along.

Thus he scarcely heard the whir of a rope through the air, and it settled over his shoulders, pinioning his arms to his sides before he was aware of what had happened. He managed a half-turn in his saddle then, seeing Consuelo take a dally around her saddle horn and whirl her horse away at an angle. The rope sang taut, lifting Chan out of his kak and bringing him thudding to the ground. Instantly Consuelo was off her horse, coming down the rope hand over hand until she hovered over him, Mitch laughing uproariously the while.

"Chan, you've usually got plenty of savvy," his foster-brother said. "But sometimes I think you must have been out behind the corral mending gear when the brains was passed out.

264

You dumb ox. She kissed me yesterday because Cazborg was closing in on me and she thought he'd kill me. It was a hero's reward for making a try at saving her. And it didn't spell a damn thing!"

"You mean — ?"

"It's been you — and nobody else but you all along," Mitch said. "Sure, I paid a lot of attention to her on the trail. That was because she'd told me that you'd asked her to marry you the first time you came to Whispering. I hated you then, Chan, remember? Every night that I was at her wagon was just another night that you had to sit by the fire and chew your fingernails down to your elbow. Hell, man, there's a red-headed gal in Amarillo that I'm thinking about. And once we get some houses thrown up in Whispering, *I'm* the gent that's taking a *pasear* to Texas."

"Mitch," Chan said, with a great show of severity, "as boss of the Lazy-L, I'm reminding you that there's work to be done back in the Basin. *Vamoose! Pronto!*"

And after Mitch had ridden away, still laughing, Chan pulled Consuelo down beside him, where she pillowed her head against his shoulder and managed to look very, very innocent.

"Then it *is* me?" he insisted, for even now this miracle still seemed beyond his grasp.

"That, too, is something the trail decide," she said. "When you first come to Montana, I want to hate you, but on the trail when I see what kind of *hombre* you are —" She sighed contentedly, snuggling closer. "You will take good care of me, *señor?* I am a *niña,* the baby who needs a big strong gringo to protect me."

And remembering many things — the bullet hole she'd shot in his sombrero, her rifle yammering on the south bank of the Red, the fuse she'd lighted slowly crawling toward a powder keg, he said sternly, "You are the *niña* who needs a big strong gringo to spank hell out of you!"

But he was smiling as he kissed her. And what did he care for all the longhorns in Whispering, or anything else for that matter, at such a moment as this one?

We hope you have enjoyed this Large Print book. Other Thorndike Press or Chivers Press Large Print books are available at your library or directly from the publishers. For more information about current and upcoming titles, please call or write, without obligation, to:

Thorndike Press
P.O. Box 159
Thorndike, Maine 04986
USA
Tel. (800) 223-6121 (U.S. & Canada)
In Maine call collect: (207) 948-2962

OR

Chivers Press Limited
Windsor Bridge Road
Bath BA2 3AX
England
Tel. (0225) 335336

All our Large Print titles are designed for easy reading, and all our books are made to last.